BY THE BOOK
The Cougar Playlist – Book 1

Sofia Gioconda

BY THE BOOK
The Cougar Playlist – Book 1

4PLAY PRESS

Chapter 1

In the Year 7953EG, in the 19th Year of the Reign of Queen Jacqueline, Vinzenza was a city holding its breath. Everyone knew dark titbits about the Order and its presumed warlocks, but the one tale everyone agreed to be true was that Lord Eduard, the young scion of House Conetti, the highest ducal house in the land, second only to the royal house, upon attaining his majority at age twenty-one, would be named Prince Consort by the Order and take his place beside the queen, a woman twenty years his senior. Lord Eduard had fostered at the palace since his early teens, but only recently had the rumours that he might be the Prince Consort foretold for over a century surfaced in earnest.

No one could agree on what, exactly, the nature of the prince consort's relationship to the queen was to be. Some whispered, after several flagons of some foul beverage, that the prince consort was to be a true husband to the queen, not a ceremonial one. Such whispers were met with mixed horror, disgust, and titillation. Truly, the prospect of the great queen, a handsome woman twice the young Lord Eduard's age, debasing herself by lying with a husband so much younger – barely even a man, really – was a topic of silent unease throughout the city.

In the days preceding the festival for the young lord's birthday, that unease erupted in small flourishes in the streets. Tempers short, suspicions high, skirmishes of honour – all had Vinzenza panting on a knife's edge. If this was true in the streets, it was triply so in the palazzo. The uppermost servants had among them sufficient information to feel reasonably certain a wedding would take place. Only the queen's most personal servants knew that, indeed, the bride was preparing to lie with her groom on his birthday and wedding night, as stipulated in the Foretelling.

The key subject of these rumours paced her chambers that day, agitated and apprehensive. Her ladies had tried in vain to get her to sit long enough to eat and drink something, but she could only alight for a few seconds at a time. Occasionally, she would look sharply at one of her ladies and demand, "Will he hate me? He will. Oh, he'll hate me," before walking away, once more muttering about allowing the Order to keep the information from Lord Eduard until he came into his majority. If he had grown up knowing – for the Foretelling had shown at his birth that he met the criteria - understanding it was inevitable, he would be able to take the role on with more comfort. As it was, he would learn all at once. They would explain that he was the product of a carefully engineered genetic mating that required his father's blood and his mother's magic to create a Perfect Consort for Queen Jacqueline, herself the product of careful breeding. As the queen's prince consort and true husband, he was to accompany her in wielding the power of Vinzenza to break the curse that had lain upon the land for nearly 300 years. To that end, he would be marrying the queen on his birthday and *taking up residence in the royal chambers as her consort.*

It would be a shock. That his birth was so carefully planned. That he was to be prince consort. That-. The idea of becoming a husband to a woman so much older, whom he knew well, would not be welcome. How could it be? Even in the relatively broad socially acceptable range of sexual practices, where men routinely took wives twenty years their juniors, women did not do the same. Such a practice was taboo in Vinzenza in those years. Even a symbolic marriage between a much-older woman and a young man would be abhorrent to the people, no matter how much it might be explained to them that only through this union could Vinzenza be saved. If they were to learn that the Order had decreed that for the magic to work, the relationship could not remain in the relative safety of symbolism, but would need to be a true coupling, they might well lose their respect for the sullied queen and her spoiled young husband and try to put them out in the streets. It was a dangerous thing the Order had demanded of her. More for her than for anyone. And yet...the tightness in the queen's stomach spread southward, a flutter of anticipation that made her squeeze her thighs together momentarily. She flushed with embarrassment. Had it been so long, that the prospect of bedding Lord Eduard made her body react so easily?

***

Lord Eduard, scion of House Conetti, sat in his chambers, enjoying a leisurely breakfast before starting the no-doubt hectic, if festive, proceedings of the day. He sat at the window, overlooking the Canale Reale, and watched the scurrying Vinzenziani preparing for the day's events, absent-mindedly worrying an orange peel in his hands. "Timak, what were you able to learn about the ceremonies this evening? What does my charming queen have planned for me?"

"I'm sorry to have to tell you, Your Grace, that if I had been able to learn, it would be more than my hide is worth to tell you. But I was not able to learn anything at all. Even asking one of the queen's inner circle causes them to go pale and dash away."

"That wicked thing!" Eduard exclaimed fondly. "What absurd thing does she have in store for me?" He turned his handsome face to the large portrait of the queen, in her guise as Defender of Vinzenza, which had hung in his chambers as long as he had been at the palazzo. The painter had captured the elegant serenity that those who knew the queen well knew to be her most defining characteristic. Eduard felt a surge of fondness, gazing at the painting now. Vinzenza's queen. His queen. His beautiful, strong, loving queen. Eduard gave a contented sigh. He'd been traveling in other parts of the kingdom finishing his education much of the time in the last three years. It was good to be back in Vinzenza. Good to know he'd be able to breathe its familiar mustiness. Good to know he would dine every night with his queen across the table, her eyes flashing and her hands dancing while she regaled him with stories from every corner of her ken and *imagination. At least, unless she expected him to marry someone and leave the palazzo.*

Eduard's smile widened. "Timak, are you able to tell me where Herself is, at least, or is that also a high state secret?" Timak flushed both with amusement and in vexation that he, HE, of all people had been utterly unable to learn anything about the ceremonies to take place that night. The very secrecy of the thing led him to certain suspicions. Suspicions he had not mentioned to his lord. Nor, he thought, had it occurred to Lord Eduard to ask.

Lord Eduard, for his part, was not so naïve as his otherwise loyal servant imagined. He had his suspicions, the queen having given birth to no heir, about some manner of symbolic consortship between himself and the queen that would be put in place until he married and the queen withdrew to leave him on the throne, with her as Chief Advisor. He was not sure of the mechanics, but he had been able to overhear enough titbits about the Order's Foretelling to suspect something of the sort, no matter how hard the palazzo and university librarians had worked to keep him from learning anything about it. It had annoyed him that the queen, for surely only she would have such power, had found it necessary to shield him from any impending responsibility he might have in breaking the curse, with the Order's guidance. He didn't fear responsibility. He was, after all, a lord himself. No, Eduard had a deep sense of duty, instilled in him since childhood by his parents and later by the queen. Eduard would rise to whatever responsibility was lain upon him.

Chapter 2

I stretched luxuriously and looked out the window. *Not bad for some introductory exposition,* I thought. In my career as an author of historical fiction, this book, featuring the story and adventures of Queen Jacqueline and Lord Eduard, was to be the first in a new historical fantasy series, and I found myself wrapping the freedom of the fantasy setting around me like a fur stole. Such freedom!

The neighbour kid, Josh, or Jason, or whoever he was, walked by outside, leading a pack of six charges, "clients" in his dog-walking business. I shook my head in wonder, because the kid probably weighed 98 lbs. wet, and here he was, attached to a good 300 lbs. of dogflesh, without a care in the world about whether someone happened to see a squirrel.

I looked back at the screen. I needed to do some research this afternoon on Renaissance Italy, which held the historical inspirations for my fantasy kingdom of Vinzenza. I had some vague impressions of canals, burgundy velvet brocades, and back-stabbing, allegedly incestuous dynasties, but that was about it. I needed to dig deeper, really get a sense of the culture, both inside and outside the nobility, so I could decide what to keep and what to change for my world. A glance at the clock had me out of my seat and headed for the kitchen. Speaking of young noblemen, the first of my Thanksgiving guests, my best friend, Sasha's, kid, was due in tonight. Sasha had called that morning to say she and the rest of the family would be arriving Thanksgiving Day because of a mix-up with the tickets. Gabe was at school just an hour away, and the food at mine being better than university food, he was still planning to arrive the day before. I knew he'd been homesick this semester, so I wanted to make sure his favourite dishes, linguine with clam sauce and a luscious chocolate torte with ganache icing, were ready to surprise him.

The sauce started, I headed to take a shower and change. Gabe had texted to say he would arrive soon, so there was just time to shower and get dressed before he got here. I adjusted the rainwater taps in the walk-in shower and eased my neck around in a slow circle under the water. The writing was going great, but I had to admit, the hours sitting at the desk, staring at that screen, were not great for my neck and back. I'd have to see if Gabe would massage my neck and shoulders for me after dinner. He'd learned to do that from a YouTube video in high school because his mom had really bad neck trouble. He quickly became famous for it through our whole circle of friends, all of us writers who spend long hours hunched over keyboards. I grinned, remembering that sweet kid who taught himself how to give shoulder rubs for his mom's birthday, and ended up getting rich in tips every time we all got together to talk shop. That first party, by the eighth massage, so had a wad of tips and was already talking about the comics he was going to buy with them. He was so earnest, the tips only got bigger after that. Yeah, he was a good kid.

And he knew it, too, the little brat. I gave a little chuckle.

A familiar voice came from the doorway. "I know the rain shower is great, but I didn't think it was a laugh-out-loud kind of thing," Gabe chuckled. I jumped and whirled toward the door, using my arm to clear a path to see through in the glass door. "Kiddo! You're early! I'll be right out!"

"Don't rush, Miriam, it's cool. I can keep you company while you finish," Gabe replied, strolling into the bathroom and taking a seat at the vanity. The opacity of the shower walls made it so only my outline from the waist up was even visible, and I wasn't particularly prude, so we were both comfortable with his staying. "I'm sure the hot water is nice on your neck after a long day writing."

"Ugh, you have no idea, Gabe. But how did you know I was writing all day?"

"My mom said you were excited about the new project because it was really different, so I checked your study first when I got here. I saw the tell-tale diet coke cans and McVitie's packet that told me you'd been at your desk all bloody day, without drinking enough water, judging by the number of diet coke cans I saw, by the way."

"Guilty as charged," I conceded. "But did you see my word count? I got a lot done already today!"

"Yeah, I saw that! That was all from today? Wow, go Miriam! I didn't read any of it. I just glanced at the word count, and then I came looking for you. Hey, is dinner almost ready? Is there anything you need me to do?"

"Yeah, it's almost ready, if you could put the water on for the pasta, that would be awesome."

"Oh sweet, are we having linguine with clam sauce for dinner?"

"Of course! My best friend's kid is sort of home for Thanksgiving. Since your family aren't here yet, I thought I could soften the blow by making your favourite dinner. I hope it isn't too disappointing to have dinner with an old lady instead of a hot girl at school."

"First of all, Miriam, you're not old. When you were in town for that conference and we went to dinner, everyone mistook you for my girlfriend."

"Yeah, yeah, they just wanted a bigger tip out of me," I answered, laughing. It was true. Recently I was in the city for a conference and figured I'd take Gabe out, since his parents were too far now to just drop in. Several people did make comments that showed they thought we were a couple. Not at all bad for my ego. Not only was he a lot younger than I, but he was also exceptionally handsome.

"Okay, I'll get the water on, then," Gabe said, heading for the bathroom door.

"Thanks, kiddo. I'll be right out," I called, reaching for the tap to turn the temperature cooler to rinse my hair.

Stepping out of the shower a minute later, I was, as usual, belting out one of my favourite shower time tunes, "Barbie Girl," while I towelled off my hair and reached for my dressing gown. A sharp intake of breath between stanzas alerted me to his presence in the doorway. I turned, asking, "So did you get--"

"Jesus, Miriam, um," Gabe held his hand out in front of him to block his view. I looked down. I hadn't tied the dressing gown sash, so when I turned, it came completely open, causing me to flash him full on. "Oh, crap, sorry, kiddo!" I laughed, scrambling to pull the gown around me and secure it. "Though you don't have to freak out so much. It's not like you haven't seen them before," I teased as I got to him, grabbing both cheeks and pinching obnoxiously. A couple years before, I had had an unfortunate episode with a toga at Halloween. I ended up flashing the entire party. They never let me forget it.

He shook free, chuckling, and wrapped his arms around me. "Hey, Mir," he said quietly into my hair. "I've missed you."

I sighed contentedly and leaned back a little to look up at him. "I've missed you, too, kid. In a way, I'm glad you got here ahead of your family, so I have time with my roomie before they get here." When Gabe's family moved, Gabe really hadn't wanted to change schools for his last two years. Since we were practically family, it was just natural for him to move in with me for those two years and take over my guest room. We were already close but living together those two years had made us even closer.

"Come with me to my room, I wanted to ask you something." I led the way down the hall to my room and went into the closet, clicking on the light. "So. . .I've been thinking about something a little daring."

15

"Uh-oh. If you think it's daring, Miriam, I'm not sure I want to know," the brat chuckled. I threw a shoe at the closet door and was satisfied to hear his answering squawk of indignation.

"Anyway," I said pointedly, "I've been thinking about trying that dating thing."

"Okay. What about it?" came his guarded reply. I peeked out the closet door and saw him standing at my dresser, arms resting on top, and his chin resting on top of them, looking at the little collection of pictures I kept there, many of which had his mom in them and various parts of the family, including him.

"I wanted your advice on the profile. You know, I want to be appealing, but not, um, slutty, and I don't want to seem like a, what is it, a catfisher?"

"Ha, a catfish. I don't think anyone is going to think you're a catfish, Miriam, but yeah, I can help you with the profile, if you want. You definitely need better pictures, that's for sure."

"You don't even know what pictures I was going to use!" I objected.

"Miriam, you've sent us two selfies in the past week. You never send selfies. I have to assume it's because of this." My silence conceded the point for me, so he went on. "They just won't do. That one makes you look like a farmer's wife, and not in a good way. And the other one is the opposite extreme. The hammock one? It kind of looks like you aren't wearing any clothes in that pic, Mir, and I just can't be okay with that."

I giggled. "It was a whim. I hadn't planned it. I thought maybe the viewer would assume I was wearing a swimsuit that just wasn't obvious through the hammock..."

"None of which addresses the question of why you were lying naked in the hammock, but I don't think I want to know," he answered quickly.

I thought back to the afternoon I had taken that new toy out to enjoy al fresco in the hammock. My God, was it hard not to scream out there in the yard for all to hear when I turned that bad boy on high. Purple Peter. I gave an involuntary shiver. That was money well-spent. "You're right," I confirmed. "You don't. Okay, so if not those pictures, will you take new ones?"

"You want me to take pictures for your dating profile?"

"Who better? You know how men will react, so you can make sure I use pictures that will strike the right tone," I argued.

Gabe was quiet so long, I thought he'd left the room. I came out of the closet, leggings on, shirt in hand, ready to go to the kitchen to give him hell for just walking out on in the middle of a conversation. But he hadn't left. He was sitting on the floor, looking at pictures on his phone. Without turning, he remarked, "You should do one picture in this dress. I like this dress." I had knelt next to the bed to pull out the sweater box in search of that new slinky sweater I'd bought, which I thought would look great in one of these pictures we were going to do. I looked up when Gabe commented on the dress.

"Which one?" I asked. He indicated the picture currently on the screen, so I crawled over toward him to see which one he meant. It was that one I loved, too, of the two of us on his high school graduation day. One of his parents had taken it. I had the same shot on my phone. It was a happy memory.

"Geez, Miriam, do that again," Gabe ordered.

"What?"

"That thing where you crawled toward me. That would look kind of hot, but not too bad. Let me take a picture of it to see." I backed away and crawled back toward him, trying different facial expressions, ranging from playful to seductive, which felt pretty weird, since it was my best friend's kid on the other side of the camera. "Uh, yeah, that should do it," he said tightly, dropping the phone to his lap.

"Let me see," I insisted, reaching for the phone. He squeaked – actually squeaked – and dove for the phone.

"No, I'll show you, I'll show you. Damn, no need to get grabby," he laughed. His eyes avoided mine. He unlocked his phone and passed it to me. I started scrolling through the pictures he had just taken.

"Ha, I just look constipated in this one," I exclaimed.

"What? Where?" he demanded, leaning closer, so close the warmth of his breath mingled with mine.

"This one," I said, pointing at the screen.

"No, you don't, silly Miriam," he scoffed, kissing my cheek. "You look great. You look...sexy. You know, other than the fact that you're my mom's best friend."

"Sexy? Really? You think so?" I asked doubtfully.

"Absolutely. And you are sexy. The problem isn't going to be attracting men, Miriam, it's going to be fighting them off," he said, standing and offering his hand to pull me up.

"There you go, sweet-talking your old roomie, again," I laughed. I had been clutching my shirt in front of me as an apron, and now turned my back quickly to slip it over my head. "I need to check the sauce," I offered, making for the door. Gabe followed me out to the kitchen and sniffed at the sauce.

"Smells good. I'm starving," he groaned.

"Hey, wouldn't it be fun if we made it fancy," I suggested. "We could light candles and everything."

"Good idea," he responded easily, looking down at his t-shirt and jeans. "I'd better go change into something a little more respectable then."

"You don't need to change, kiddo. You look perfect just as you are. Very handsome." I reached out and unfolded the cuff of his t-shirt sleeve, which had gotten folded up in the back. He moved toward the hallway in the direction of his room.

"Be right back," he called from halfway down the hall.

Chapter 3

Scowling, the Monsignor stood at his desk looking over the Canale Central, and the palazzo on the other side of it. He pondered the ceremony that would take place that night, joining the whore queen and the sunny brat of a ducal house. Did the woman think she would call his bluff about the Foretelling that he and three other members of the Order would have to witness the consummation of the marriage? The Monsignor paused a moment to gain control of the reaction his body had to that twisted anticipation. Yes, for the politics to play as he intended, the physical act had to be witnessed by Order members who could be relied upon to betray the trust of the Order and carry the news to their respective duchies.

In short order, those three sons of goats would sow the seeds of disgust against the queen, and her power would diminish until she became a boneless puppet in the Order's – in his – deft hands. The Monsignor permitted himself a half-smile. Yes, before long, the Order would have total control of the kingdom's three duchies and the crown, and he, as the chief orchestrator, would be at its head. He turned his back to the palazzo and left the room to prepare himself, spiritually and physically, for the feast, and its aftermath.

***

Smoothing her hands down her sides and over her belly, the queen surveyed the royal chambers with a critical eye. When she returned, it would be *with her new husband, who would likely hate her. She had arranged everything carefully, to be as comfortable to him, as familiar, as possible. She'd applied gardenia perfume, of which Lord Eduard had been fond since he first came to foster at the palazzo. During these recent years of so much travel, every time he came back to palazzo, he would kneel, as was appropriate, in greeting, before accepting her warm hug, burying his face in her neck, and inhaling deeply, commenting that her perfume was the most soothing in all the world. He'd straighten, laughter in his eyes, hand over his heart, and say rakishly, "Your Highness, you smell most enchanting," with exaggerated courtly manners.*

"Mathilde, do you see anything amiss?" Mathilde, the one person alive who could, without fear, tell the queen she had MISSED something, cast her critical eye around the room, and then along the person of the queen herself, head to toe. She reached out to change the hang of the queen's many pendants here, and tuck an errant lock of hair away there, before nodding in satisfaction.

"It is all as it should be, Your Majesty." As Queen Jacqueline's personal assistant and trusted friend, Mathilde understood like no one else the worry the queen was experiencing, so afraid that her young husband would truly hate her once he learned, that he would be disgusted. She reached out her steady hand and rested it on Jacqueline's shoulder. Two maids who saw drew in their breaths sharply. "Your Majesty, he won't. He won't hate you. He never could," Mathilde murmured next to

21

her mistress's ear. *"He never could."* She repeated with finality. The queen maintained her forward gaze and her ramrod stiff posture for a moment before cutting her eyes to glance at Mathilde.

"Just so, Mathilde. From your lips to the ears of the gods. From your lips..." before taking a deep breath and continuing her exit from the chamber.

***

The banquet hall, was, of course, a madhouse, so Eduard was able, with relative ease, to sneak along the edges and make his way into one of the side kitchens, the chief domain of his favourite pastry chef, Michele. He'd backed into the kitchen, careful not to be observed, when he felt a solid object pressed into the small of his back. A low, growling voice said, *"You have three seconds to explain what you're doing here before I beat you senseless and add you to a stew."*

Eduard chuckled softly, *"Ah, Michele, I know well you would never be able to bring yourself to do it."*

Michele grumbled menacingly. *"You keep trying my patience, lordling..."* before something soft thwacked Eduard across the back of the head.

"Hey, what was that for?" The young lord turned to laughingly glare at his childhood friend. *"And where is my special treat?"* Michele lowered the rolling pin and dropped the towel he had used to strike his friend. Shrugging one shoulder, he indicated a corner shelf.

"They're over there but mind you don't eat too many. Herself would know where you got them and have my ear." Eduard looked up, half a tart already

22

crammed in his mouth. "Mmpphf, Mmmfee," Eduard pronounced regally. Michele raised an eyebrow.

"I assume, based on knowledge gained over the infamous years of our acquaintance," sighed Michele, "That you are admonishing me to relax, like the spoiled brat lordling you are."

Eduard grinned, brushing crumbs from his beard. "Besides, Mich, I'm a 21-year-old man. How would I get full on such a modest little peccadillo?" He clapped his friend affectionately on the shoulder. "And now I need to go seek out Her Royal Highness the Queen, to further my efforts to learn what on earth she has planned for tonight, the little minx. Thank you, Mich." Eduard strolled from the room, no longer concerned about being seen. Some servants hurried to get out of his way, while others, mirroring the nobleman's nonchalant attitude, merely strove not to run the young man down.

As Eduard entered the main hall, he spotted the queen's entourage heading away from him to the left and hurried to catch up. "Your Highness! Slow down, I beg, you winged woman! I want to talk to Your Highness, if I may!" Finally, he caught up to her, clasping his chest and pretending to pant dramatically. Having captured the Royal Hand, he brought his queen's fingers to his lips in greeting. "Good afternoon, my radiant queen," Eduard teased quietly. "Where has Your Highness been all day?"

The queen smiled warmly at her ebullient subject. "I, Lord Eduard, have been exactly where my duties dictated I be." She arched a playful *eyebrow and lifted her fingers to brush a crumb from his face. "Can you say the same?" Eduard flushed a boyish pink at being caught out, though his queen would have known even without the crumbs, he suspected. The woman always knew.*

He broke into a winning grin. "Well, my constant duty is to attend to my queen, of course, Your Highness, even on my birthday, I might add, so I am here, looking for you, just as I should be." Eduard folded his arms and looked at the queen with impish insolence. The queen fought not to laugh, clearing her throat to gain control.

"Yes, well, I'm glad you're here. I wanted to ask you why it is your man, Timak, has been taxing my inner circle in a most unsubtle manner trying to get information about the ceremony I expressly forbade you to ask about?" The queen swatted Eduard's arm with mock severity. "And don't you dare allege that you didn't tell him to, or that his doing so on your behalf means you did not break the terms of my orders." Eduard had the grace to look mildly sheepish.

Chapter 4

I stirred the sauce and put the pasta in the boiling water before getting candles and candleholders out and setting them on the table. It occurred to me to ask Gabe if he wanted me to open a bottle of wine to have with dinner. Wiping my hands dry on my shirt, I moved toward his room to ask.

His door was ajar when I got there. He was shirtless. Damn, when did he develop that kind of muscle tone? Gone was the skinny kid I met when I first met his mom and became instant friends with her. Somehow, he had grown into a man. A beautiful man, too. He'd obviously been working out more this semester. He had taken off his jeans and had khakis out to put on. He was looking down at his phone and muttering, so I moved a step closer, ready to knock on the door to announce my presence. I was raising my fist when he groaned, "Fuck, my mom's best friend, really? Of all the women I could want, fucking why?!" His other hand drifted down his stomach. He was scrolling through pictures on his phone. "How am I looking at this picture and calling it sexy, what is wrong with me?" he grumbled. "Fuck, though, look at you." His hand drifted down further. I felt dirty for witnessing this, but I was right next to the squeaky floorboard, and I was terrified if I took a step now, he would hear, and he would know I saw and heard. Gabe sat down on the edge of the bed, still staring at his phone, his other hand fully inside his boxer briefs and gripping himself. He swiped through a few more pictures. "Christ, taking pictures of her in the shower, too," he said, "Thank God she didn't get to those when she was looking at the crawling ones." His strokes became more rigorous. "God, I'm a sick fuck. Why are you so sexy to me, Miriam?" he said in a tormented voice as his pulling at his cock got more intense. I should not be looking at this and hearing this. I should at least close my eyes if I couldn't walk away. But I couldn't. I was mesmerized by the sight of Sasha's beautiful boy, whom I'd known since he was a pup, talking to my sexy pictures and jerking off vigorously, not knowing I was right there watching. My hands, pressed flat against my stomach, crept lower down my abdomen. I could feel... damn it, I could feel I was wet *down there*. Creepy, but at least no worse than Gabe, eyes screwed shut now, head back, pumping his cock rapidly, and just mouthing, "Miriam, Miriam, Miriam," over and over. Fuck. One hand had found its way inside my panties and was pinching my clit hard. I wasn't going to be able to eat dinner like this. As Gabe shuddered and spent inside his boxer briefs, I used the moment of distraction to hurry away and headed for my room to use Purple Peter for just a quick minute before dinner, to take the edge off. I could not possibly eat dinner with him calmly right now, without releasing some of this pressure.

My hands shook only slightly as I lit the candles a few minutes later, after my quickie session with Purple Peter in my room while dinner finished. Gabe came out, looking achingly grown-up, and remarkably unflustered. "Wow, candles and everything, huh?" he chuckled, coming up behind me and placing a sweet kiss on the top of my head, as he'd taken to doing while he was living with me. I thought it was a sort of protective gesture. Sweet boy.

"I told you I wanted it to be special," I responded, hoping to keep the quaver out of my voice. "I think everything is ready now. You pour the wine. I'll serve." I hurried toward the kitchen, struggling still to calm my racing thoughts. I served the food quickly, trying to be mindful to keep the presentation at least a little special.

"Hey, Mir, do you need help carrying stuff out?" Gabe asked, surprisingly close to my ear.

"Oh! Gabe, I didn't even hear you come in!" Warm hands came down on my shoulders and turned me.

Gabe searched my face, brow furrowed. "You okay, Mir?"

I tried unsuccessfully to hit a light tone. "Yeah, kiddo, I'm fine. Can you carry this, and I'll carry the plates?" I thrust the salad into his hands, avoiding his gaze. I followed him into the dining room and set everything down. Dinner was an exercise in striving to find our usual easy camaraderie. My mind was awhirl, and given what I'd seen, I knew his had to be, too. Where had this come from?

"I didn't tell you, there's a surprise!" I managed, with forced lightness to my tone. Gabe's eyebrows shot up. Yes, fair, there had been plenty of surprises already. "There's a special dessert," I clarified, standing to get it.

"You want me to get it, Miriam?" he asked. "You put in all this work."

"Oh no, you don't, mister. It's a surprise. I'll get it," I said over my shoulder as I made my way with the pasta bowls to get the cake. I took the cake – his favourite, dark chocolate with a ganache frosting – from its hiding place in the fancy china cabinet, checking the sliced strawberry garnish to make sure it was in place, and heading back out to the dining room. When he saw it, his eyes lit up, exactly as I knew they would. I set the cake down and took a moment to enjoy his expression before cutting it. He looked up and broke into a grin.

"Uh, Miriam, you've got-" he indicated his nose with a fingertip and dropped his eyes to the cake, chuckling. Frosting. Of course. I had frosting on my nose. And the cheeky brat was all too happy to tease me about it since I had a gift for getting frosting somewhere on my face every time. I swiped at my nose irritably and came away with a streak of the rich ganache on my finger. Without thinking, I popped my finger in my mouth to suck the frosting off.

Immediately, the energy in the room changed. It was as if Gabe had lasered in on my mouth, watching me suck the frosting off while something I didn't understand crackled almost visibly in the space between us, both of us aware, at least, of what he had done just before dinner, though he didn't know I had seen. Unable to resist, I pushed my finger further into my mouth, eyes locked on his. I made a small, contented sound in my throat as I pulled my now-clean finger slowly from my mouth. "Oops," I said softly. "Not sure how I always manage to do that." I gave a little chuckle as I set to cutting slices of the cake.

Gabe shifted in his seat and cleared his throat. "Yeah, you seem to have a knack for it," he commented, avoiding my gaze. "So, uh, tell me about this new project, Miriam. It seems like it's coming really well," he asked. The book. Yes. That was something solid to stand on. That was something that didn't terrify me. I took refuge in it.

Over dessert, I told Gabe a bit more about my new project, a historical fantasy inspired by Renaissance Italy, with the Medici family and their ilk. It had struck me as a time-place not used enough in fantasy, and full of interesting challenges for a writer. As I talked, we both relaxed into the comfortable dynamic we'd always enjoyed while I spun tales in the air for him.

After cake, we carried the dishes into the kitchen. Gabe pulled his phone out and put some music on while we worked together to clean up. REM came on, "Shiny Happy People," one of my favourites, and without realizing it, I started to dance as I tidied the last things away. Before long, I felt the warmth of a body behind me. Gabe was dancing behind me, singing along with the song. I turned and took his hands, laughing. We danced around the kitchen, giggling, and enjoying each other's company.

The song changed, Robert Smith's voice overtaking Michael Stipes' voice to send the sensuous lyrics of The Cure's "Pictures of You" into the kitchen, as Gabe smiled down at me and pulled me closer, folding one arm behind me, caging me into his embrace in the new dance. One hand on his chest – this new, grown-up chest he had developed – I happily followed his lead, letting him twirl me around the kitchen island. The giggling had faded now, each of us lost in complex thoughts. I felt his body reacting, stirring against my belly. His breathing, and then mine, became shallow. Rather than pull away, we instinctively moved together, closing the last distance between us. No longer dancing around the kitchen, we were more swaying in place, staring at each other. "Miriam," he whispered, lowering his head to rest his forehead against mine. We stilled, our ragged breath comingling between us. "Miriam," he said again, sounding tormented.

And then he was gone. He released me from his arms and left the kitchen so fast, I heard the front door slam before I even processed the fact that he'd gone. I braced my hands against the kitchen island, gulping air. What the fuck was that? Tears of angry confusion flowed freely down my face. Sasha's kid. Sasha's sweet, gentle, kid, who had somehow become a man without my realizing.

My best friend's kid, who was out there, hurting, and needed me to fix this somehow. Furiously wiping the tears from my face, I headed for the door, grabbing both of our jackets, as well as the stadium blanket, from the cloak closet before heading out into the November night after him. I knew where he would go. Since he was little, Sasha and Tim had taken him for star-gazing parties at the baseball field attached to the high school, a couple of blocks from their house and just up the street from mine. After Sasha and I met, I was often at their house for dinner, or they were at mine, so I went along on the excursions. We'd spent happy hours there together, one of us sometimes carrying Gabe, and later, his brothers, home when he fell asleep waiting for the late-night constellations to come up. It was his place of comfort. When his first girlfriend broke up with him, Sasha found him there, lying in the outfield, staring at the night sky. The night before he went off to university, when he couldn't admit he was scared to leave home, essentially for the second time, I'd found him, and the missing half-bottle of rum, lying in the outfield, waiting for me to come and tell him it was going to be okay.

Tonight was no different. As I neared the field, I saw his lithe form stretched out in the usual spot. I slowed my pace and approached gently. I spread the big stadium blanket out, holding his jacket out to him silently before lowering myself to lie on one side of the blanket. He slid the jacket on wordlessly and zipped it up. After several minutes, I offered softly, "Wanna talk about it?"

For a while, I thought he might not answer. Finally, he spoke, haltingly at first. "What was that, Miriam? What the fuck is wrong with me? You're. . .you're my mom's best friend. You're – and don't get me wrong, you're gorgeous – but you're old enough to be my mother. You're practically

31

family." His voice cracked slightly. My heart ached for him.

"Nothing, Gabe. Nothing is wrong with you," I soothed, reaching out for his hand, and lacing our fingers together. "You've been away at school. Your parents are across the country. There's been a lot of change, and we've always been close. For the last two years, it was just us roomies, so we got even closer. I think it's perfectly natural."

He snorted derisively. "Yeah? You think my friends at school went home and got hard-ons for their moms' friends?" he asked bitterly. My mind raced, trying to find the path to make this okay for him.

"To be fair," I said dryly, finally, "Their moms' friends probably aren't as hot as me." I gave his hand a playful squeeze. Total silence made me afraid I'd miscalculated, but then, as I'd hoped, that golden sound came to my ears. Laughter. He was laughing. I'd managed to break the tension. His laughter grew stronger, the tension melting away. I couldn't help joining him. What a ridiculous situation. My best friend's kid jerking off to my pictures, getting hard dancing with me... me getting turned on by all of it, which he didn't know, fortunately. . . Using our laced hands, he pulled me to him. I cuddled into him, resting my head on his chest, just as he'd so often done on mine.

"Sorry, Miriam. I guess I'm kind of a perv, and kind of a drama queen," he chuckled into my hair before kissing my temple.

"I guess we have that in common, huh?" I responded, chuckling in response. We lay there a while longer in comfortable silence before he finally got up and reached down to pull me up.

"Let's go home," he said, "It's cold as fuck out here!" We folded up the stadium blanket and made our way home, arms around each other. "You still want me to watch that documentary with you tonight?" he asked as we turned onto the walk up to the front door. I'd mentioned earlier that there was a documentary on the Medici that I wanted to get watched as part of my research before the rest of his family arrived for Thanksgiving.

"Yeah," I said decisively. "That would be helpful. I know I won't have time to work on it again until after everyone goes home Saturday."

Chapter 5

A perfunctory tap at the door brought Jacqueline out of her troubled reverie in time for her to look up to see Eduard stride into her chambers confidently. "There she is," he crooned playfully. "The most beautiful woman in the Nine Kingdoms." He plucked her hand from where it fidgeted in her lap and pulled her gently to her feet, his brow furrowed. "But what troubles you, Your Highness? It's the night of my birthday feast! Surely, matters of state can be fretted over tomorrow?"

The queen allowed herself a moment to enjoy Eduard's embrace, revelling in his mutually comforting habit of nuzzling her neck and inhaling her scent deeply. His contented hum reverberated through her body. Would he still nuzzle her and take comfort in her after the kingdom's needs demanded that he become her husband tonight? He would do his duty. He had been raised to revere his duty to the kingdom. Too well, she thought now with bitterness. If he were less duty-bound, she might be less fearful of losing his affection tonight. The kingdom might be doomed to fall to the curse if he did, but at least she would have this sweet boy among her closest subjects.

"Come, Your Highness, your people wait. I'm sure they're hungry." An audible grumble from Eduard's stomach made them both laugh.

"And not just them, it seems," the queen remarked, one eyebrow quirked. "Did Michele feed

you so poorly when you snuck down to the kitchens?" The young lord adopted an expression of aggrieved dignity.

"Your Highness, that was hours ago. I am a young man just entering my majority. I need to eat more often than that," he grinned. Straightening, Eduard smoothed his hands over his own hair before tucking a lock of the queen's hair that had been dislodged in their embrace back into place. "Come," he said grandly, offering his arm. "The feast awaits." The queen drank in a last, long look at his innocent face as she took his proffered arm.

"Yes," she agreed with forced cheerfulness. "Your feast awaits." Lord and queen made their way together down to the banquet hall, passing scurrying, liveried servants, and occasional clumps of bowing guests. They came to a stop before the doors of the hall, waiting to be announced. The queen looked over at this happy young man, so confident and comfortable in his place in the world. "Happy birthday, Eduard," she murmured. Eduard grinned.

"I thank you, Your Highness. Let's go celebrate." He led her into the hall, supporting her by the elbow as she climbed the three steps onto the dais and moved to take her place at the centre of the table. The hall quieted as she and Lord Eduard took their places at the table. The queen raised her hands in greeting.

"Good evening to you, everyone. We are pleased to share with all of you the occasion of Lord Eduard's attainment of his majority. I invite you to eat well, drink deep, and toast the good

health of Lord Eduard as you enjoy the hospitality tonight." The queen took the goblet being held discreetly in waiting by a servant. "To Lord Eduard," she toasted, turning to him and holding her goblet to his to toast him. "May you live long and wisely."

The toast was met with a general cheer, and all assembled drank to Lord Eduard's long life and wise council. The meal was served in scores of exquisite dishes. Courtiers came to offer gifts. Bards played and sang pieces of varying quality commissioned for the occasion by the palazzo, the couriers, and sovereigns of neighbouring kingdoms wishing to send their greetings. Because of the curse, none had been able to breach the borders of the kingdom in either direction for hundreds of years, but there were still means of communication. With rumours rife that at last, there was real hope of breaking the curse, communiques from the other kingdoms had come much more often.

Jacqueline and Eduard were carefully watched throughout the occasion for signs of what might happen, making it impossible for the queen to have a frank discussion with her future husband. Nonetheless, she was able, by titbits dropped among other exchanges, to warn him that the marriage would take place, and there was no real alternative. Eduard, having been raised to a high role, betrayed no shock beyond a few brief widenings of the eyes with his face turned away from the crowd toward his queen, and even these, he brought under control as soon as they occurred.

With a small curve to her lips and a majestic tilt to her head, the queen acknowledged and dismissed another well-wisher, adding quietly, "You understand what I've told you, what is being demanded of us?" Only Eduard could see how fearful she was of his reply. With a kindness and a wisdom beyond his years, made possible by his deep love for the queen, Eduard consciously packed away any qualms, knowing that his queen would have thought of his concerns already. His primary concern became the protection of her, with the breaking of the curse coming somewhat behind. He blinked slowly and treated her to the slow, cocky chuckle she found so endearing.

Taking the wine pitcher from the nearby servant to pour the queen's wine himself he said quietly. "It will be as you say, Your Highness, and I will be a lucky man, with the loveliest wife in all the Nine Kingdoms." He returned the pitcher to the servant and waved her away. "Please stop being afraid," he added. "You are somewhat older than I, which is unconventional. But you are truly the greatest beauty I have ever seen, and will continue to guide me with your wisdom as my revered wife, just as you have always done as my revered queen. I could never object to this union." He lifted her hand to his lips. "We will find our way."

Eyes locked on Eduard's, the queen drank from the goblet, relief washing over her in waves. She gave a slight nod. "We will find our way," she echoed. "It is time." She waited for his nod, and stood, bracing herself. She waited for silence and offered her hopes that everyone had found sufficient enjoyment in their meals. "Tonight, Lord Eduard's birthday also marks the beginning of the end of the curse within whose shadow the kingdom has been trapped for generations. It has been foretold by the sages of the Order," here the queen turned to nod briefly to the Monsignor at the end of the table, "That the bloodline of House Conetti and the magic of the Vindrene Sisterhood, combined, would produce a Perfect Consort to rule at the side of the Queen of Vinzenza and banish the curse for good and all."

Excited whispers and murmurs broke out here and there in the hall. The queen raised a regal eyebrow and waited pointedly for the hall to return to silence.

"We are aware that this Foretelling, while not widely known in detail, has been the subject of no small amount of speculation and rumour, though we are confident, of course, that none of our loyal nobles here assembled have participated in any of the more salacious threads of rumour-mongering that have made it to our ears." Again, the queen raised an eyebrow, indicating that she was no such fool as to be confident of any such thing. She allowed her gaze to light briefly on a few whom she knew to have been particularly gleeful in their drawing room musings. Important to remind them that she had ears everywhere, and if they'd gotten away with their disrespectful talk, it was because she had allowed it.

"Tonight, Lord Eduard, Son of House Conetti and the Vindrene Sisterhood, having reached his majority at the age of twenty-one, [|] *takes his place at*

my side as that Perfect Consort." The queen looked at her intended, who was looking at her with such serenity and love, it filled her with the strength to continue. "Lord Eduard," she addressed him. "This night, I would take you as my Perfect Consort, to rule this land at my side and banish the curse from it at last. Do you accept?" They had not rehearsed, since he didn't know ahead of time, but she knew his instinct and upbringing would lead him sufficiently well. Lord Eduard did not disappoint his queen. Eyes slightly wider than usual, looking into the stormy grey eyes of his queen, Eduard took her outstretched hand and knelt on one knee before her. Voice pitched to be heard throughout the hall, Lord Eduard responded, eyes never leaving hers, "Queen Jacqueline, it is my honour to accept your proposal and take my place at your side as your Perfect Consort. For the good of the kingdom, my body and soul are yours to guide. Will you take me as I am and guide me in ruling at your side, my queen?" For a long moment, the feast hall fell away. Queen and lord communed through their eyes in an eloquent conversation of trepidation, trust, and affection.

The queen nodded, tears glistening in her eyes, and responded, "I will."

Chapter 6

Returning from the baseball field, we hung up our jackets and set about getting ready to have our pyjama party. Gabe went to the kitchen to make popcorn. He joined me in my room, where I'd pulled the film up on the big screen I'd moved in there after he left for school in August. I emerged from the closet in my customary little sleeping t-shirt and shorts, heading for the bathroom to perform my ablutions. Gabe set the popcorn on the dresser and disappeared from the room. A few minutes later, I was at the sink, dancing to my night-time playlist while washing my face, when he appeared in the doorway, still in his dressy clothes, toothbrush in hand.

Gabe gave me a wolfish grin in the mirror. "Sing it, Miriam!" he encouraged, egging me on. Patting my face dry with a towel and reaching for my moisturizer, I hammed it up for comedic effect, wiggling in place and singing along with Lady Gaga while applying the cream. He had his phone in his hand, and declared, "Yeah, that's actually a really cute picture of you for the profile, Mir," he said, holding the phone toward me to show me. I blushed.

"You took a picture of me washing my face in my pyjamas?" I squawked indignantly, smacking his arm. "Brat!" He chuckled insolently and dodged away from my playful blow. I examined the picture. It was kind of cute, I had to admit. He had a good eye. I swiped to the previous image, the one he'd taken before dinner, of me crawling toward him. I guessed it was pretty hot. That was also the picture he'd been looking at while jerking off before dinner... a tightness started to gather in my belly. *Swipe.* Another couple of images from my room, and then, one I hadn't seen before. Was that-? It was. It was my outline, in the shower, when he first got home. He must have included this when he had his cock gripped in his hand before dinner. Without meaning to, I squeezed my thighs together. Quickly, I swiped back to the most recent image. "Yeah, I guess that's pretty cute. You think that's what men will find attractive?" I asked doubtfully, holding the phone out to him. He looked down at the image, an expression of gentle fondness on his handsome face.

"Yeah, Miriam, I do. Quit being like that. You're gorgeous. You have nothing to be insecure about." His eyes met mine in the mirror. He set his phone down on the counter and started his ablutions. He was just spitting out the rinse water when Right Said Fred's "I'm Too Sexy," came up on my playlist from the bedroom. I had forgotten I'd added it one night as a joke. I grabbed my hairbrush from the vanity and sang along, grabbing Gabe's tie and backing into the bedroom, pulling him with me. "He's too sexy for his tie, too sexy for his tie, so sexy, my my," I sang. His low chuckle increased the tightness in my belly as I reached up to loosen his tie while singing along. By the time the song ended, we were breathless from laughter, and he'd exchanged his tie and dress shirt for a pyjama shirt. He turned to unbuckle his belt so he could change into pyjama pants and reflected in the closet door mirror, I couldn't help but notice as his khakis came down that his boxer briefs were tented by a full erection. I looked away, my mouth drying. Just ignore it, Miriam. You just ignore that, is what you do. I crawled onto the bed and busied myself with the remote while he finished changing and made whatever...adjustments he needed to make. Gabe grabbed the popcorn and settled himself with his head at the foot of the bed, lying on his stomach.

"Okay, tell me what we're watching here," he said, once he was comfortable, or as comfortable as he could be, lying on the erection he had hidden under himself. "Anything I need to know going in?"

"Let's see. This is about a dynasty in one of the Renaissance Italian cities I've used as inspiration. The Medici were a 16th-century political dynasty in Florence. Very wealthy. Very powerful. They produced four popes and two queens of France. Great patrons of the arts. Some very strong women. Supposedly incestuous, because, you know, popes, queens, strong women. People envied them. I'm combining inspiration from them with the historical Venice, with its canals and doges."

I hit play and we started watching what turned out to be a remarkably dry treatment of a fascinating subject. Gabe frequently interrupted to ask questions, which I didn't mind, since he was more interesting anyway, and especially so in this case. By the halfway point, we were just talking over the film, him lolling alternately on his back and his side, no longer watching the screen. Occasionally, when I got carried away on some tangent or another, he would playfully nip at my leg, positioned as he was with his head toward the foot of the bed. After the fourth or fifth such indignity, I broke off with a shriek of mock outrage. "Oh, that's it, brat! I've spoiled you for too long!" I pounced and tickled him. So adorable that this big strong grown-up man was as ticklish now as he'd always been.

The tickling gave way eventually to sleepy giggles, and when the film, which we mostly hadn't watched, ended, we'd already fallen asleep on top of the covers, popcorn forgotten and toppled off the side of the bed, with me snuggled into Gabe's armpit, my head on his chest, his hand tangled in my hair.

With the first soft rays of November sunlight peeking around the corners of the blinds, I snuggled deeper into my warm cocoon, wiggling contently into the warmth at my back. And the delicious, rigid promise pressing against my ass. How I had always loved that feeling, pushing back against a warm body and a hard cock in the morning. I luxuriated in the dream, grinding slowly back into my dream partner. It felt so deliciously real, I thought. What a great dream. Gradually, the fog of sleep began to clear, and memory started to flood back. Gabe. Gabe here early for Thanksgiving. The pictures. The sexual tension. Gabe jerking off before dinner looking at my pictures. The dancing. The tickling. Gabe was the warm body behind me. That cock pressing against my ass with his. What the fuck was wrong with me? I had to get out of this bed. Had to get into the shower before he woke up. His family would be arriving in a few short hours.

43

And yet. As I started to ease out of the bed, Gabe made a little noise of protest and pulled me more closely against him with the arm that had been thrown over my waist so loosely until I started to withdraw. I settled back against him, giving in, rubbing my ass against his impressive morning wood. He moaned quietly in his sleep. Fuck. Just a couple more wiggles against him, and then I'd get up. My left hand drifted down my stomach, to the waistband of my sleep shorts. I couldn't, though. Couldn't indulge myself so far. Could I? "Mmm, Miriam," Gabe murmured sleepily into my hair as he pulled me closer against him in his sleep. My hand dipped into my shorts, unable to resist the pulse of need there any longer. Where was the harm in just stroking a little? How long had it been since I'd had a man in my bed? I dipped a finger into myself, surprised to find myself already well lubricated and ready. A hum of pleasure sounded in my throat. Behind me, Gabe had started to awaken. I could hear the change in his breathing. Any second, he would realize where he was, and with whom. I would have to feign sleep. His breathing quickened more. He was awake. He remembered. He must. And yet he hadn't pulled away. "Miriam?" he whispered, barely above the sound of a breath. I stilled. "You asleep?" he asked. Still, I didn't answer. I'd let him get out of bed and into the shower, or into his own room, whatever he needed, without knowing I was awake to share this continued perversion.

He didn't move away. On the contrary, the arm that had pulled me to him tightened, pulled me against him harder. He began to move against me, grinding his erection against me. "Fuck, Miriam," he moaned softly. His fingers toyed with the waistband of my shorts.

"Gabe? You're awake?" He stilled. "No, it's okay…don't stop. Please?" A heartbeat passed. I half-expected him to leap up and flee the room. Instead, he buried his face in my hair and groaned.

"Fuuuuck, Miriam," he moaned. He gripped my hip, fingers toying with my shorts restlessly, panting against my neck.

"Pull them down," I urged, "It's okay. I want you to," I added, raising my hip to pull the other side of my shorts down below my ass, signalling more than simple acquiescence, active participation. Equal responsibility. Growling with feral urgency, he yanked the side he had access to, baring my ass to him, allowing our bodies to touch flesh to flesh.

"Oh, goddamn, Mir," he groaned, his cock sliding along my asscrack, lubricated generously by his pre-come. I was panting, with desire, with need, with the building orgasm that promised to shake me to my foundations. His hand smoothed upward along my stomach to cup a breast, making me whimper quietly. His hand tightened on my breast, two fingers cradling my nipple, pinching gently. His pelvis moved more quickly, his breathing growing more laboured, his face buried in my neck, inhaling deeply the scent of my hair. "Mir, Mir, oh fuck Miriam," he was saying, chanting, almost like an incantation. Both of us, instinctively, without conscious thought, increased our speed.

My hand, two fingers in my pussy, thumb rubbing feverishly at my clit, cramped with the effort, but I couldn't stop. My release was building. It was almost within reach, and it was beyond my ability to deny it now. "Oh, Gabe, don't stop. Please. Please, don't stop," I managed to moan as the waves started to crest and envelop me. I cried out, writhing against him. I felt his release as he shuddered against me, coating my ass with a slick mess of his come. Still, I couldn't stop. Kept riding the rolling waves of ecstasy, gradually slowing, until I was limp, boneless, sated.

Almost in unison, our breathing and pulses slowed. With that slowing, reality crept back, as well. Pressed against him as I was, I felt the moment when Gabe fell victim to the doubt and disgust that had plagued him the night before. Wordlessly, he started to back away. I turned, still in the warm cage of his body, and pinned him in place with my gaze. For what felt like half an eternity, we searched each other's eyes. Finally, I stretched up to kiss him on the nose. "It's okay, kiddo," I said simply, before rolling over and out of bed, headed for the shower.

Chapter 7

Vows exchanged, when Eduard rose, he kept his queen's – his wife's – hand in his and brought his lips to hers in a tender kiss. As one, queen and lord, wife and husband, they turned to face their nobles. Eduard had been raised at court. He knew the queen – and now, by extension, he – had enemies at every rank. He knew some would disregard the Order's Foretelling and declare any union between a woman her age and a young man barely having reached his majority a depravity that must not be accepted. He squared his shoulders and let some of his usual joviality fade from his face and posture. He would do his duty, and more importantly, he would protect his queen. No chink would be found in the armour of their union.

With his other hand, the Perfect Consort raised his goblet. "We ask you to join us in a toast to our union, to our queen. May she live long and continue to reign wisely." He brought his goblet against his wife's and used to cover of bringing the cup to his lips to wink at her reassuringly. The queen bowed her head slightly in acknowledgment and smiled softly as she lifted her cup to drink. One challenge was met. The wedding ritual was simple and had been completed. According to the laws of the land, the queen needed no authority other than her own for the marriage to be legal, so the simple exchange of intentions sufficed. Her new husband had accepted the marriage gracefully and was not angry with her. She only hoped he would be as forgiving about the consummation once faced with the reality of it.

Renewed by the excitement of the marriage, the feast continued for hours. Musicians played and people danced. The queen and prince consort descended to the centre of the hall to dance three dances together, the first just the two of them, the others among other dancing couples. Many guests fell asleep where they sat, either unwilling to open themselves to criticism by leaving early or simply enjoying themselves too much to want to go.

Finally, the queen judged it was time to withdraw. She waited for Eduard to finish his exchange with a drunk noble who'd come to congratulate him and leaned toward him, turning her head so her lips could not be read. "I believe it is time for us to withdraw, sweetling. Shall we bid our subjects goodnight?" In answer, Eduard took his wife's hand and brought her up with him as he stood. They each held up their non-clasped hands to call for quiet. Once satisfied that all those who were awake, including many who had been nudged back to wakefulness by their neighbours, were paying attention, the queen spoke.

"The prince consort and I thank you for your unflagging loyalty and your congratulations on this important day. We retire now, but welcome those who wish to stay to do so with Our blessing."

Jacqueline moved her hand forward, palm out, in a gesture of blessing, and nodded slightly as she saw Eduard hesitatingly raise his free hand to mirror her gesture. Closing her eyes, the queen gathered the magic around her, pulling it from the atmosphere and spooling it inside herself, letting it flow into Eduard through their clasped hands enough to let him know he should gather the magic to him, as well. A shimmering aura formed around them, bright and steady, feeling warm against their skin. Slowly, guiding Eduard through their connection, the queen sent tendrils of magic out to touch those gathered, guest and servant alike. Peace settled upon the crowd, as the comforting warmth touched each mind and eased the worries and fears within. Gradually, Jacqueline and Eduard released the magic back into the air and finally lowered their hands. Servants came forward to move their heavy chairs away further to allow them to walk to the end of the dais. Eduard went one step ahead so that he was below the queen as she descended the steps. At the doors, he took her arm, just as he had to enter, and led her through the palazzo toward the royal chambers.

Entering the chambers, both allowed their shoulders to slump in relief. The Queen turned to her husband, concern etched on her features. "I'm sorry I didn't tell you, Eduard. The Monsignor insisted that none outside the Order know apart from myself, and even that much seemed to vex him." The prince consort paused in the process of removing the belt that held his ceremonial weapons.

"I suspected that was the case, Your H-, uh, Jac-, er, my sweet, and it was hardly a surprise. Despite the Order's best efforts, and the restrictions the Monsignor somehow dared to place upon you, I was able to glean some information about the Foretelling and what it would likely mean when I

reached my majority." He grinned boyishly. "It's no great hardship to be married to the most beautiful woman in the Nine Kingdoms, who also happens to be the wisest and kindest."

The queen flushed with pleasure at the compliment and opened her mouth to speak, but was prevented by the opening of the door leading to the adjoining sitting room and the appearance in that door of the Monsignor. "I'm so glad to hear you say so, Your Highness," the Monsignor oozed. "May I extend my heartfelt congratulations on the success of your nuptials thus far?"

Eduard schooled his features and answered the Monsignor coolly, gathering the hauteur of royal privilege around him like a cloak. "We thank you, Monsignor. I am sure we did not look to have your congratulatory visit at so late an hour, nor," he looked pointedly around him, "In so intimate a setting." The queen's breast swelled with pride at her young husband's adroit handling of the Monsignor, though she feared this time, it would not be enough to gain the upper hand.

The Monsignor's self-satisfied air warned her that he intended to make good on the threat he had made the day before concerning the consummation of the marriage. The Monsignor insisted that not only would the marriage have to be consummated for it to be useful in the ending of the curse, but that someone, presumably the Monsignor, the stinking perverted maggot, from the Order would need to witness the act, both to quell murmurs of doubt and to satisfy a vague and heretofore unmentioned

50

aspect of the Foretelling. The queen suppressed a sigh.

"We give you leave to speak of the matter you have come here to address, Monsignor," she said coldly. The Monsignor's unctuous smile broadened, and he sketched a bow so shallow as to be insolent. "I thank you, Your Highness, I will," the Monsignor gestured with one hand, and three members of the Order emerged from the sitting room to flank him. "As we have discussed, it is necessary that your ... union be consummated for it to be effective in breaking the curse." Jacqueline could see that Eduard had gone pale next to her and she moved closer to him so she could lay a comforting hand on his arm.

"Yes, Monsignor, but it hardly seems necessary to discuss now, so late at night," the queen began, but was cut off by the Monsignor's hands coming up in a gesture of false supplication.

"Forgive me, Your Highness, but I assure you it is only that very necessity which could bring me to impose our presence upon our sovereigns under such circumstances. You see, upon consultation with the Oracle, I have concluded that it would be best for a delegation from the Order to witness the consummation. I'm afraid it is the only way." The Monsignor's head lowered in apparent apology, but both Jacqueline and Eduard knew well his bowed head was concealing a hateful smile. Only the queen's lifetime of court training made it possible for her to keep her composure. She had hoped to discuss this topic with Eduard in private, hear his views on the matter, and come to a mutual

51

understanding. Somehow, she would have to persuade the Monsignor to allow them some privacy so she could reassure him. To her surprise, it was the prince consort himself who spoke.

"That is what the Oracle indicates, is it, Monsignor?" The Monsignor, recovering from his surprise that the prince consort had spoken first, made to reply, but Eduard held up a staying hand, reaching his other out to take his wife's hand. "We will allow this witnessing," declared the prince consort coldly, "For the sake of our people. The queen and I have never shied from our duties, and we will not do so now simply to punish your impertinence. You will allow us to perform our ablutions, first, of course, and remove our court dress. You may go. We will send for you when we are ready for you." The Monsignor looked in shock at the queen, looking for some sign that this was planned. The queen raised a haughty eyebrow.

"I believe you will find that the prince consort and I speak with one voice, Monsignor, as is appropriate. We will, as he said, send for you shortly, at our pleasure." She turned from him in a sign of dismissal, displaying a confidence of being obeyed that neither she nor the prince consort felt in that moment. Calculations flitted across the Monsignor's sharp face.

"An excellent plan, Your Highnesses," he said finally. He started to withdraw back to the queen's sitting room.

"No," cracked out the queen's voice sharply. "As my husband instructed, you will await our summons outside the royal chambers." The queen

fixed the Monsignor with that gaze that had brought many to their knees in tears. With a deep sigh, the Monsignor conceded the skirmish and left the royal chambers, the three members of the Order in his wake.

Chapter 8

Once we were up, the day became a whirlwind of preparation. Last-minute prep of guest spaces. Chopping. Getting the turkey into the oven. Making a fancy charcuterie board. Somehow, combined with the customary excitement-stress of the holiday, the shared orgasms that morning had, for the moment, at least, dispelled the awkwardness of the situation, and we moved in concert like a well-oiled machine. At 2:30, Gabe sauntered into the kitchen, where I had just finished preparing the roasted sprouts for their final, last-minute jaunt through the oven. He grabbed a rosemary walnut off the top of the dish before I was able to slap his hand away and grinned. "I just got a text from my mom. They'll be here in about half an hour. Get out of here and go get dressed." His cocky grin as he tried to get past me to snag another walnut from the dish stirred the butterflies in my belly pleasantly.

"Crap, really? Half an hour?" I smoothed my hair, taking stock of how much disorder I was in. "Yeah, okay, I'll just hop in the shower to rinse off and get dressed. Thanks," I said, as I hurried toward my room. I took a lightning-quick shower and set about getting dressed before the chaos hit with the arrival of Sasha, Tim, and the kids. I wiggled into a bra and panties and started toward my closet to find the dress I had decided to wear. I tugged the hair tie out of my messy bun, sending my hair tumbling around my shoulders in disordered waves. Gabe appeared in the door of the closet as I took the dress off the hanger.

"Oh, yeah, you look great in that dress, Miriam, good choice," he said. I looked over my shoulder at him and my breath caught. He'd changed into his dressy clothes already. So handsome. I eyed his tie and remembered playfully leading him from the bathroom to the bedroom by that same tie the night before. The immediate pebbling of my nipples at the memory had me regretting the choice of an unlined bra. Fortunately, the closet was too dark for him to see from where he was. Something in my demeanour must have given away my agitation, though, because he closed the space between us, his brow furrowed in concern. "Hey, Mir, what just happened? What's wrong?" His hands rested on my shoulders as he searched my face.

"No, it's nothing, kiddo. I'm fine," I assured him. He gently took the dress from my hands and unzipped the back before bunching it at the sides and holding it over my head. He jerked his chin at my arms, indicating that I should raise them. When I did so, he eased the sleeves onto my arms and over my head. He pulled the dress into place and turned me by the shoulders, so my back was to him.

"I don't think your nipples even show through the dress," he said quietly into my ear. I whirled and smacked his arm, laughing.

"You weren't supposed to see!" I protested.

"Yeah, well, I'm not sure how blind you think I am, gorgeous," he responded in his best Humphrey Bogart voice. "There was no hiding those beauties."

He threw his arms up to defend himself from my onslaught of laughing smacks.

"Such a brat! I can't believe you!" I exclaimed, continuing to smack at him ineffectually until he grabbed my hands.

"No violence on Thanksgiving, Miriam," he said sternly, before breaking into a wide, playful grin. He kissed my forehead and released my hands. "I think the chaos is starting." He made it to the bedroom door before the doorbell started ringing cacophonously. I heard him throw open the door and start greeting his family.

Thanksgiving was a success. Gabe, having lived here the last two years, was a sort of co-host, always attuned to where I was and what I needed help with. Sleeves rolled up, always ready to pitch in and fully participate in our hosting of the holiday. The day was spent in semi-controlled chaos, with everyone talking and laughing, eating and generally having a great time.

Gabe's brothers were staying in the guest room that had become his room, since there were still two beds in there. Gabe had moved to the study, which adjoined my room, to sleep on the surprisingly comfortable couch in there. I crawled into bed, grateful to be able to rest after such a busy day. I was so tired that I almost – almost – didn't think about what had happened when I was last in my bed. A hot pulse between my legs as I remembered it signalled my body's vivid recollection of that morning. Disappointing, that he wouldn't be sleeping in my bed tonight. I sighed and turned out the light.

I lay in the dark, fantasizing like a depraved pervert about my best friend's son lying on the couch next door for a good while before the door to the study opened quietly. Gabe stood uncertainly, outlined in the moon's light. "You awake?" he asked.

"Yeah, kiddo, you okay?" He moved toward the bed.

"The, uh, couch is kind of lumpy," he lied. I grinned in the dark.

"You're welcome to sleep in here, then, if you like," I replied, unable to keep the smile out of my voice. Needing no further invitation, he climbed into bed and lay on his back next to me. I rolled onto my side toward him. "Thanks for all your help today, roomie," I murmured. He grinned and his arms gathered me to him and pulled the covers up, pulling my head down onto his chest. I settled into him and hummed contentedly. He absently toyed with my hair as we lay in the darkness.

Unable to resist, I teased quietly, "If you're going to play with my hair, you could at least do me the favour of pulling it." I giggled against his chest.

In answer, he tugged gently on my hair to lift my head while his fingers found my chin and tipped my face up toward him in the darkness. His mouth found mine in a searing kiss unlike any I had ever experienced. I kissed him back, surprised, confused, hungry. Eventually, he pulled back, panting. "Careful what you tease," he whispered against my lips. "Now go to sleep, naughty roomie. Everyone is going to want their Morning After Thanksgiving Cinnamon Rolls bright and early whether you've slept enough or not." I gulped a few deep breaths, knowing pushing it any further was out of the question, cinnamon rolls or no, and settled my head back onto his chest to sleep.

In the morning, I had no illusion that I was dreaming when I became aware of the erection pressing into me from behind. I had turned in the night and was nestled against Gabe as the little spoon, his cock pressed insistently against my ass. I smiled into the mostly dark room and rotated my hips to rub against him. Apparently, he was already awake. "Fucking finally," he growled very quietly in my ear, reaching for the waistband of my panties and yanking them down. The arm that was under me wrapped around to push me back against him while the other hand made its way, with surprising confidence, downward to cup my pussy. He buried his nose in my hair and inhaled deeply. "Holy fuck, Miriam," he breathed, thrusting a finger into me as he ground his cock against me. I gave a tiny whimper and reached back to grip his hip and pull him to me harder. "Shhhh," he admonished. "We have to be really quiet, Mir. We can't let them hear." The pace of both his fingers in my pussy and his hips humping me increased with his breathing. I bit my lip, knowing how right he was that we absolutely could not allow ourselves to be heard. He kept whispering, "We can't let them know that I'm in here with my cock between your asscheeks and my fingers fucking your pussy while the house is full of my family."

Fuck, the way he injected so much glee into such a filthy statement. My body went stiff as my climax started. I inhaled sharply and might have cried out, but the hand that had been on my chest came up quickly to cover my mouth. He was right, of course, but in that moment, in protest, I bit his stifling hand, just as I felt him spend against me. He nipped my ear. "I can't believe you BIT me, Miriam," he whispered. "I'll make you pay for that." He chuckled. I shivered. He dislodged his other hand from my pussy and smoothed it up my belly, smearing my juices along my flesh as he did so.

With a final grind back against his softening cock, I threw my legs over the side of the bed and stood. "Race you to the shower," I whispered and headed into the bathroom. Somehow, we managed to shower, together, without making noise. I went out to the kitchen a few minutes ahead of him, to avoid suspicion, but his brothers were watching cartoons in the other room, oblivious to anyone else, and Sasha and Tim hadn't come out yet. Working together, we got my famous Morning After Thanksgiving Cinnamon Rolls into the oven before the boys came stumbling into the kitchen in search of sustenance.

I'd always loved having the house full at Thanksgiving, and I loved spending time with Sasha and her family, but I was keenly aware all that day – and that evening – that I just wanted them gone, wanted them to leave me alone with Gabe, who would be going back to school on Sunday. I feigned exhaustion as early as was reasonable and made for bed, waiting impatiently for him to get free of them and do the same. Almost as soon as I heard the study door close behind him, I slipped out of bed and made my way to the connecting door.

I stood in the doorway, wondering what the hell I was doing. Gabe had just changed into pyjamas and was sitting on the couch, looking unsettled. "Everybody in bed?" I murmured.

He looked up and grinned. "Yeah, I think so, though probably my brothers are playing videogames under the covers." I crossed to the couch and sat next to him.

"Yeah, I guess that's their thing, huh? I think you were always more of a book and flashlight under the covers kid." Gabe chuckled and nodded, moving slightly closer to me. "I always have been, too," I went on, "Though it's been a while since I've had to hide under the covers to read all night."

"I still do it," Gabe said, "Even though there's no one to hide it from. It's. . .comforting somehow. In fact, the, um, the last book I read under the covers like that was one of yours." He ducked his head shyly. My mouth came open in surprise. I moved closer to him without even meaning to.

"Really?" I asked, looking up at him. He looked down at me and gave a wolfish grin.

"Really," he confirmed, lowering his head so his lips hovered just above mine. Our breath comingled as we sat in the darkened room, breathing shallow, hearts racing.

"Do you, um, want to sleep in my room again, since the couch is, um, lumpy," I asked with some effort. He lowered his mouth to mine and gave me a long, sweet kiss.

"That would be really great, Miriam," he responded. He stood and took my hand, leading me back into my room. We climbed into the bed and lay there looking at each other, tentatively exchanging soft kisses and caresses. Gradually, my eyes got droopier and droopier. Eventually, I fell asleep, snuggled against Gabe's chest.

The next morning, before our new ritual, Gabe half-sat and pulled his t-shirt over his head. "Before you come," he whispered, "Cover your mouth with this to keep yourself quiet." He chuckled softly. "As hot as it was when you bit me yesterday, I'm not sure I can explain a second bite on my hand today." I blushed and nodded. When the time came, inhaling his scent as I stuffed his shirt against my mouth intensified the sensory experience to a degree that the shirt nearly rendered itself self-defeating.

After a final lunch, Sasha and Tim herded the boys into the rental car and headed for the airport, leaving us alone again, finally, by dinner. "What do you want to do tonight, Mir?" Gabe asked, coming back into the house after we waved off his family. I looked up from the bottle of wine I was opening and then let my gaze drop to the two wine glasses I had already gotten out. Once filled, I handed him a glass of wine and held mine up to clink against it.

"I thought we could order take-away and just relax tonight," I replied before taking a deep draft of my wine and dropping my eyes toward the floor, trying not to think about his imminent departure the next day. He ducked his head to capture my eyes.

"Hey. Hey, Mir, what's wrong?" He set his glass down and took mine from me to set it on the counter before gathering me into his arms. I sighed and let myself melt against him, wrapping my arms around his waist. He pulled back and looked down at me. "Is it because I have to go back tomorrow?" I nodded, feeling guilty at the same time for making him worry. He pulled me back to him and rested his head against mine. He held me silently for several moments before delivering, with an audible smile in his voice, a line his mom and I had both used on him so many times over the years. "Let's not borrow trouble. That's not until tomorrow." We chuckled in unison. I swatted his arm gently.

"Smug brat," I declared fondly. "All right, brat, what are we going to order in? We can Netflix and chill tonight." He had picked up his glass and was taking a drink when I said this, which led to his choking and coughing. "Um, Miriam, what do you think 'Netflix and chill' means?" he asked with mock severity. I blinked.

"Just what it sounds like. Staying home, chilling out, and watching something on Netflix," I responded patiently.

"Yeah, no, Mir, that's not – that's not what that means. Promise me you won't say that to anyone else," he laughed. I thought about the possible implications of what he was saying and felt myself blush scarlet.

"I see…" I buried my face in my hands, laughing. "Okay, good to know. Glad it was just the two of us when I said that." He looked up from his phone, where he was perusing the Indian takeaway menu.

"Me too, Miriam, believe me. You want to share the chicken jalfrezi and the veggie korma, as usual?" I watched his face while he placed the order, suffused with fondness for him.

"Sounds perfect, kiddo."

When the food arrived, we shared it while half-watching another Renaissance Italy documentary and mostly chatting about the book and his schoolwork and what his Christmas break plans were. We fell asleep cuddling, with the lights still on.

Both of us awoke early, when dawn was just lightening the sky. Gabe had his arms around me, holding me tightly against him. His cock was already hard against me. I grinned and reached behind me, squeezing his hip. I took hold of the waistband of his boxer briefs and began to ease it down. A growl rumbled through his chest, and he lifted the hip that rested on the bed to allow me to pull the waistband lower, and lower, freeing his cock to press against me. I lifted my hip off the bed, and he grabbed my panties in the centre in the back and tugged them down urgently, his breath ragged against my hair. "Oh, fuck, Miriam, yes," he moaned when I reached between us to take him in my fist. He bucked against my hand several times before removing his arm from around me and rummaging under his pillow. His sharp intake of breath, my squeezing of his cock, and the *whirring* of an electric appliance coincided to give me a sharp rush of adrenaline. "Hey," he said, with slight hesitation. "I thought, maybe, is this okay?" He brought one of my vibrators, the little pink one that was far more powerful than it looked, out from under the pillow. I grinned and squeezed his cock harder.

"Very okay," I purred, anticipation making my voice husky. He groaned and brought the toy down between my legs. I released his cock to free my hand to guide him. I started by guiding his hand in teasing my clit with the head of the vibrator. My head went back as I writhed back against him, moaning. "Fuck, yes, that's good," I breathed. Gabe ground his cock against me, following my lead as I guided his hand back to stroke the vibrator along my slit. It slid easily, my body eager to welcome it. I whimpered, already chasing my climax.

"Fuck, Miriam, you're so wet," he moaned, plunging the vibrator easily into my pussy. I cried out.

"More," I demanded. "I need more." He increased his speed, fucking me actively with it without further guidance. My breath was coming out in sobs as I climbed closer to orgasm. "Gabe, oh God, yes," I cried out, trembling, the waves of sensation so intense, it was as if I was trying to escape further stimulus. Gabe pulled it out and tossed it on the bed, not taking time to turn it off. Gripping my hips, he turned me wordlessly so I was face down on the bed. He wrapped one arm under me to hold me to him and resumed feverishly running his cock along my ass, sliding further and further forward until the head of his cock rested almost at my entrance. "Gabe," I gasped, desperately wanting to let it happen in that moment, but worried that he'd regret it deeply. "I don't think-

" He growled in frustration but moved back up again, and two strokes later, with a savage yell, he released control and came, slowing his movements as he softened against me before collapsing next to me on the bed. We spent a minute catching our breath, and then I turned to face him, propping myself up on one elbow. My other hand roamed leisurely over his chest in a soothing circular motion. Finally, he spoke, conflicting expressions warring on his face.

"I'm sorry I almost-" I laid a finger over his lips to still them.

"Stop," I ordered quietly. "There's nothing to apologize for, and believe me when I say stopping you hurt me more than it hurt you." I chuckled self-deprecatingly and took a deep breath. "You didn't do anything wrong, kiddo. I have no idea what this is and where it's going. But I swear to you, you have nothing to apologize for. We're in this together." For a long time, he continued to stare at the ceiling, avoiding my gaze. Finally, his eyes sought mine.

"Okay, Mir. Thanks." My heart filled with affection for this sweet, beautiful boy – sweet, beautiful man, now.

I kissed him on the cheek. "Come on, let's get some breakfast going. I'm starving, for some reason." He gave me a smug, wolfish grin.

"I'll bet you are," he chuckled. We kept breakfast simple, using some of the leftovers and finishing with pie, as was customary for post-Thanksgiving weekend meals. After, we bundled up and headed out to the hammocks in the backyard for some last quiet time before he had to leave. There were two hammocks, but after he climbed into his and settled into it, he reached for my arm and pulled me to him playfully. I laughed.

"I don't know, kiddo. Are you sure you want to pile in together and risk it?"

He laughed and pulled harder, unbalancing me so I toppled inelegantly into the hammock, half next to him, half on top of him. His arms came around me. He nuzzled the top of my head and murmured, "Mmm, you smell good."

"Yeah? What do I smell like?" He made a show of smelling my head carefully. I could hear the smile in his voice when he spoke.

"I guess a lot of it is your shampoo. Grapefruit and rosemary, mostly. And then the part that's just you. Smells like... well, smells like home." He rested his chin on my head and we lay there contently for several moments before he spoke again. "I have a theory, you know," he remarked.

I craned my head to look up at him. "A theory about what, kiddo?"

"About why you were out here naked in the hammock." I blushed.

"I see. And what is your theory?" I asked. He repositioned me so I was on top of him. I instinctively spread my legs to straddle him to keep us from tipping over.

"I think that you came out here," he lowered his voice to a dramatic whisper in my ear, "To touch yourself like a naughty, slutty roomie." His hands slid up under my shirt as he spoke. My cheeks heated instantly because he was right, of course. I

66

had brought my new toy out and fucked myself with it in the hammock, legs spread and dangling over the sides. And here I was a month later, on top of Gabe, with his cock hard against me and his thumbs flicking my nipples to attention.

He noticed my reaction and his gaze sharpened. "Oh, shit, I was mostly kidding. Seriously? That's fucking hot, Miriam." Gripping my hips, he moved so that the evidence of how hot he thought that was pushed against me exactly where we both wanted him to be, with only our clothes in the way. I moaned softly. We looked into each other's eyes for long moments. "Miriam, I—I should go. I—yeah. I should go." He looked away, confused and conflicted. I let him wiggle out from under me and roll out of the hammock. I stayed there while he went inside to gather his stuff, letting the tears flow unchecked, waiting for them to dry on my face before going back inside to see him off.

Chapter 9

Once the door closed, the prince consort turned to his wife and began, "I-" the queen pulled him to her in a firm embrace and breathed into his ear.

"We have not swept for Listeners, Eduard. We must assume they can hear us," she warned. The prince consort pulled away and gave her a sweet, confident smile.

"I was only going to say, my lovely wife," the prince consort continued, undaunted, as he started to pull the pins from her hair and set them on the decorative table at his hip, "That I hoped my things had been moved into the royal chambers already, as I would like to have something more comfortable to wear while we prepare ourselves for our. . .rest." He lowered his lips to hers and whispered against them, "We will not give them the satisfaction of sharing our private misgivings with them, my beautiful and wise wife." He kissed her softly, wrapping her in his embrace more closely as he deepened the kiss. Her heart full of admiration at her husband's courage and dignity of spirit, the queen melted into his embrace and kissed him with an outpouring of her affection for him.

"Come," he said aloud, "Let us retire and call for the tiresome clerics so that they may look their fill and leave us in peace." He guided her into the bedchamber itself. Eyes never leaving hers, he waved away the servants who had emerged from the shadows to help them undress. Piece by piece, Eduard removed the rest of the pins from his wife's

hair, and then her jewellery and other adornments. She lifted her hands to start unlacing her bodice, but he took her hands in his and lowered them gently back to her sides. With deft fingers, he unlaced her bodice and lifted it gently over her head. He pulled at the laces at the sides of her gown until they were loose enough that he was able to ease the gown back over her shoulders, letting it fall to the floor in a pool on the floor. He took her hands and helped her step over the pooled gown, leading her to sit in her short shift on the edge of the bed, eyes wide and breathing shallow. While she watched, Eduard slowly undressed himself for his bride.

"Timak," the prince consort called softly over his shoulder.

"Your Highness?" came Timak's immediate answer from just outside the doorway.

"Tell the Monsignor he has a very few minutes to attend upon his sovereigns if he wishes to be present for the consummation," the prince consort ordered.

"At once, Your Highness," replied Timak without hesitation, proud that his lord was refusing the Order the satisfaction of controlling the circumstances any more than was strictly necessary.

Eduard climbed onto the bed and lay on top of the bedclothes. "Will you join me, my queen? Forgive the presumption. Bedclothes over us might prove a point of contention, so I thought maybe we would remove the problem on our terms." Fighting a smile, Jacqueline crawled across the bed to Eduard.

"Such a clever boy," she murmured. "You have been taught well." His answering chuckle brought her smile to life, the magic sparking in the air around her. She settled herself against the prince consort's body, one hand on his chest. He lowered his mouth to hers. At the door, he heard Timak clear his throat to announce his presence.

"Are they here, Timak?"

"Yes, Your Highness."

"Good," answered the prince consort, lifting his mouth from his wife's only enough to speak. "They may enter and stand at the foot of the bed for ten minutes, and then, if they do not leave, have them removed by force, if necessary."

"Yes, Your Highness," Timak replied, his tone suggesting that he should very much like for the Monsignor and Order members to resist the time limit.

The queen allowed herself a wolfish grin of her own as she looked up at Eduard. "Taught very well indeed," she affirmed with a chuckle, as she pulled his head back to hers. The sound of rustling cloaks came through the door and came to a stop at the end of the bed. "You are not to speak," the queen commanded, "Any of you. You have your orders. Ten minutes, and then you will go, or be held in defiance of the Crown." She allowed Eduard to pull her into his embrace and gave herself over to the power his kisses held to maintain their collective control over what she had feared would become an untenable situation. She felt her husband's erection growing harder against her stomach and felt her body responding. Apparently, the schoolboy *fondness he had long displayed extended neatly to their new intimacy. Her breathing grew ragged as acceptance burned into desire. "Eduard," she breathed pleadingly into his ear.*

In answer, Eduard gently rolled her under him, working her shift up only enough to enable him to enter her in one slow, even thrust, not wanting to expose any more of her body to the eyes of the odious Monsignor and his toadies than strictly necessary. Once buried in her body, he stilled, kissing her cheeks and eyelids tenderly, letting their bodies grow accustomed to this new connection. Without being conscious of it, Jacqueline and Eduard had begun gathering their magic to them, so that, to the observer, it was only just clear through the aura surrounding them that they had, in fact, consummated the union physically. Eduard began to move, with achingly gentle thrusts, supporting his weight on his elbows. The magic built around them and inside them, warming them and heightening their senses. The prince consort's movements grew more urgent, the magic pulsing with each thrust, brightening as they both neared their climax.

"Jacqueline?" Eduard gasped, barely able to contain his orgasm. In answer, the queen dug her fingers in her new husband's flesh.

"Now," she demanded. With a soft cry, he thrust hard into her and felt her muscles constrict around him as her triumphant answering cry burst forth from her throat. "Eduard," she gasped, as he rolled onto the bed and pulled her onto her side to

71

face him. She stroked his face and chest and arms wonderingly.

"Eduard, that was very deftly handled. They can have no complaint that we failed to comply with the Oracle's supposed indications." The prince consort answered with a chuckle and reached over his wife to pull bedclothes up to cover her. Unnecessarily, his gaze swept the room to be sure Timak had seen his orders carried out. Indeed, he and his wife were alone in the room.

"Very well-done, yourself, my wife," he responded playfully. He stroked a hand down Jacqueline's flank and kissed the tip of her nose.

"They did not reckon with how very much like you I am when they sought to outmanoeuvre us," he went on. "I wonder how many more times the Monsignor will underestimate us before this is through." The queen smiled sleepily and settled her head on Eduard's chest.

"It hardly matters, sweetling. We will defeat them at every pass." With smiles on their royal faces, the queen and her foretold Perfect Consort, having faced with great success and satisfaction the first test of their union, drifted into a comfortable sleep.

The days after the wedding was a whirlwind of meetings, some with the Order, but also with groups of nobles. Some of the nobles were loyal to their sovereigns and eager to offer any support they could to the union and the efforts to break the curse. The queen and prince consort met with these in their own apartments, showing the favour of intimacy, using that intimacy to shore up their

72

political capital against the Order and those nobles who did not support them. Others came with more questionable agendas, looking for evidence of discord in the palazzo that might be exploited.

In particular, the queen summoned to them those who, outside the Order, knew most about the curse. In this way, she and Eduard prepared themselves to take on the Order and take control of the breaking of the curse. With the enormous step of the union having been taken, more of those experts seemed willing to share what they knew, taking the political risk inherent in tacitly disregarding the Order's authority. Steadily, a set of theories about the actual mechanics of breaking the curse began to take shape.

The Monsignor, aware that he was being outpaced at his own political game, continued to try to find some weakness in the royal couple. Twice, he summoned Eduard to the Map Room for "consultations," intending and hoping the prince consort would come alone so that he could be more easily manipulated. So far, they had outmanoeuvred him, but if he could get control of the boy, the Monsignor thought he, at least, could be controlled, once outside the clutches of the vile queen.

In response to the first summons, Eduard arrived with Jacqueline at his side, accompanied by several stern-faced nobles. The second time, Eduard sent a single line expressing regret that he was not able to join the Monsignor that day, being occupied, along with the queen, with state affairs. The Monsignor still hoped to bring the monarchy down, taking their place at the helm of power, but they were resisting.

The Monsignor found himself thwarted repeatedly in his efforts to seize control. Jacqueline and Eduard were inseparable since the marriage. Any hope that the new prince consort might be angry and alienated by having been kept ignorant about the marriage until his birthday was gone. If Eduard did harbour ill-feeling, it was not toward his queen, and he was too well-trained in politics to let it show. Both Eduard and Jacqueline gave all impression of being perfectly content with the arrangement.

***

The theory was straightforward enough. If the curse could only be broken by the union of the queen and the prince consort, it stood to reason that the actual breaking of the curse would be best effected by the physical presence of the couple – and their magic – at the epicentre of the curse. The queen had only once visited the site. Eduard had never seen it in person, though he had read descriptions.

The theory – or at least, the hope, was that the combined, amplified magic of the sovereigns, amplified by intimate congress, would somehow overwhelm the curse. No clear guidance was given in any of the existing studies of the curse, so there seemed little point in delaying the attempt. Unspoken was the concern that they had no way of knowing whether there was any risk in failing at the first attempt.

Chapter 10

I hit Save and reached for my wineglass, only to find it empty. When had that happened? I chuckled. Thirsty work, writing so-called "smut," I thought, no matter how well that smut was dressed up in historical fiction elegance. I made my way out to the kitchen for another glass of wine and a much-needed break.

Since Gabe went back to school Sunday, I had holed myself up in my office, working hard on the project to make up for the time I'd taken off for the holiday week. I'd been working like a woman possessed, and it was deeply satisfying to have finished so much of the book so quickly. Of course, if I were honest, I would acknowledge that I had worked with such obsessive focus to keep my mind from wandering to other topics. I could hardly be accused of avoidance, though, ignoring worries about doing sexy things with my best friend's kid by writing a fantasy novel in which a queen and the much-younger scion of a ducal house need to marry and have sex to save their kingdom from a centuries-old curse.

Sipping my wine, I made my way through the house, taking stock of the tasks I had been neglecting all week. Coming to Gabe's room, I peered in to see what disaster, if any, his brothers had left in their wake. It wasn't as bad as it could have been, but I saw several cups and an empty plate lying around that the little slobs hadn't taken out to the kitchen. The plate was on the floor next to the bed, and a piece of pie crust had been brushed off the plate to lie next to it, just under the bed. I dropped to my knees in annoyance. "Do you want ants, guys?" I asked into the air. "Because this is how we get ants." I gathered up the piece of crust and a few other crumbs and put the plate on top of the bed to take out when I left the room. Next to where the crust had lain, I noticed a stack of magazines, or – no, not magazines. They were, I discovered as I pulled them out from under the bed, lingerie catalogues. I flipped through them and noted the dates. I had just stumbled upon almost two years' worth of teenaged Gabe's version of a porn stash. I chuckled to myself. The catalogues all bore my name. He had been pilfering them all those months, so I seldom even saw them. I paged through the top catalogue, which was two years old and had been handled more than the others, by the look of it. The catalogue fell open to one page in particular that bore fingerprints indicating it was a favourite.

In my pocket, my phone chirped. I pulled it out and saw that Gabe was calling me on FaceTime. I opened the connection and settled myself cross-legged on the floor, back against the bed, grinning in greeting. "Hey, kiddo! How is your week going?"

"Not bad," he responded easily. "I wanted to tell you, though, I just sent you some material by email. Some stuff related to one of the research questions you mentioned." I was a lucky lady, to have a hot, young research assistant.

"That's great, kiddo, thanks. That was really nice of you. I've been working my ass off on that project all week."

"We certainly don't want *that* to fall off," muttered Gabe. I raised an eyebrow.

"I appreciate your concern for my ass, Gabe," I said sardonically.

"Hey, Mir, is that my comforter behind your head?" I turned my head unnecessarily.

"Oh, yeah, I'm in your room," I replied.

"Um, why, exactly?" he asked, his face displaying a this-oughta-be-good expression. I chuckled. This could be fun.

"Oh, you know," I said casually, "I just came in here to clean up after your brothers." I allowed a brief pause. "But you will never *believe* what I stumbled upon." Gabe's eyes sharpened.

"What did you stumble upon, Miriam?" he asked a little nervously, making me giggle. I picked up the top catalogue and brought it up to show the camera.

"I stumbled upon a whole stack of *these*," I chortled. Gabe covered his face with a hand.

"Okay, Miriam, God, you don't have to keep waving it around, I get the point," he groaned. "I guess there isn't any point telling you I read them for the articles, is there?" I laughed.

"Pretty sure these don't have articles, kiddo, so I'm afraid not. I notice, too, that there are some definite favourites in here. . ." I teased, earning another groan. "There are even, oh, Gabe," I laughed, as I continued to page through the top catalogues. "There are even what seem to be. .

.spills of some kind on some pages." By this point, I was laughing so hard, my stomach hurt.

"Miriam," Gabe said, trying to sound stern. "Will you please put those away? I can't believe you're-. I mean, yeah, I can, because you're my little mischievous roomie, and you're punchy because you've been writing hard for several days, and there's no amount of silliness you aren't likely to pull at this point." He gave in to my influence and started laughing with me. "Anyway, I gotta go. I have class in a minute. I just wanted to let you know I'd sent that stuff and, you know," he trailed off, embarrassed.

"And what, kiddo?" I asked softly.

"And see how you were," he finished, after a brief hesitation. "Things were confusing and sort of, um, weird when I left. I wanted to make sure you were okay." Tears pricked my eyes, and I gave him a watery smile.

"Yeah, I'm fine, Gabe. Really. It was just so nice having you all here," I sniffled. "As for the other stuff, I don't. . . I don't pretend to know what's going on there. But don't you worry about me. I'll see you before you fly home in a few weeks for Winter Break."

"So, you're not coming for Family Weekend, for sure?" he asked. "Right, you did say, before, about the book. I forgot," he said with studied casualness. He had invited me when he was at the house for Thanksgiving, since his parents couldn't fly in for a weekend again so soon. At the time, it seemed perfectly sensible to decline, so I could get writing done. I was regretting the decision somewhat now.

"I should probably stay home and work," I confirmed.

"My roommate's parents aren't coming," Gabe commented. "He's heading off to the mountains for the weekend with his girlfriend."

"Oh, yeah, so you'll have the room to yourself? Nice. You going to have a party?" I teased. "You could even have a girl spend the night, kiddo," I joked. My laughter drowned out his response, so I had to ask him to repeat it.

"I said," he said softly, "That I *had* been going to have you spend the night. Now, I really have to go to class. Later, Miriam." He disconnected. I had gotten to my feet when it hit me what Gabe had been telling me. "Little pervert," I said fondly into the room. Gabe had just told me he had the room to himself because he wanted me to be with him in his bed. I sat down abruptly on the bed. He wanted me to be with him in his bed. My blood ran hot. I looked around the room, this space that was so essentially *him*, and eased myself backward further onto the bed. I gathered the pillow to my face and breathed deeply. Mmm, sweet boy. I lay back against the pillow and brought my hands up to cup my breasts. Since I'd been writing intensely all day, I hadn't ever put a bra on. I pinched both nipples firmly, making me hiss at the pleasant sting. "Gabe," I moaned softly. I tried squeezing my thighs together, but it wasn't enough. Hooking my thumbs into my panties, I shoved them off and let my legs fall open. The cool air of the room hit my swollen clit. I took it between two fingers and pinched it hard, hips coming up off the bed in response. "Gabe," I moaned into the room.

I slipped one finger, and then another, into my pussy, raising my hips to meet my hand. I hadn't done this since he left, even after the interlude in the hammock. My body's reaction was swift. Desperately, I pumped my fingers into myself, gasping and crying out freely. Within a few short minutes, waves of pleasure were crashing over me. I screamed into his pillow, inhaling his scent.

Panting, I started to come down from my orgasm, fingers still resting in my folds, twitching. Reality crashed back as the high faded. I was on Gabe's bed, having just fucked myself, because his little porn stash, and teasing him about it, made me too fucking horny to even go to my own room. Fuck. What the fuck was wrong with me? Did I just need to get laid that badly?

I thought about the few messages I had exchanged with guys on the dating app after I finally decided to post my profile the night Gabe went back to school. There was one, Marc, who was cute, and he was in the city. Actually, he was right near the university, and he had invited me for dinner and drinks this weekend. I hadn't answered yet. I supposed I could go, have dinner and drinks, fuck him to get this out of my system, and then have lunch or something with Gabe on Saturday to soften the blow of my not going for Family Weekend before coming home to work on the book for the rest of the weekend. I pulled up the dating app on my phone to set it in motion before I lost my nerve.

I pulled up the thread of messages Marc and I had exchanged and hit Reply. *Dinner and drinks tomorrow work for me. Do you know Napolitano's, on Pecan? Shall we meet there at, say, 7? Looking forward to it. -M*

There. I'd made a date. The first date I'd made in a couple of years. Those years had been harder for my libido than I'd realized. My shaky laugh rang hollow in the room. I could do this. I'd just, well, wash this bedding I just came all over, for one thing, and then maybe go to the mall and grab something sexy to wear to boost my confidence. I glanced down at the catalogues. Yeah. Maybe something like one of the little ensembles in there, and a pretty dress. . .perfect. I'd meet Marc, enjoy his company, get laid, and whether I wanted to see him again or not, at least I wouldn't be on such a hair-trigger that this kind of nonsense with poor Gabe continued.

Three hours later, I staggered in the door, grumpy, tired, and in need of a drink. I'd found an adorable designer dress, and the same bra and panty set that I'd seen on of Gabe's favourite pages in the catalogue I looked through before going. If he thought that one was so great, probably Marc would, too. More importantly, I thought I was pretty smoking hot in it, with and without the dress, so it would give me confidence for the date.

I was too tired to get into a potentially sensitive phone call after braving the mall and shopping, so I decided not to call Gabe to tell him about the date. I knew he worked Friday mornings, so I decided I would go to his work to surprise him, take him out to lunch and tell him about the date, and then shower and get ready in his room, which was right near the restaurant. Seeing him before the date would probably help me feel more confident, as well.

When I walked into the coffee shop the next morning, a pretty blond was the only one behind the counter. Gabe must be in the back. I knew he'd been given a lot of responsibility already. He might be back there doing inventory or something. I felt a swell of pride and affection. I got my drink from the blond, whose nametag pronounced her to be Cassidy, with a smiley face before and after, and took a table tucked in a corner, where I pulled out my laptop to read some of the material Gabe had scanned for me at the library while I waited for him to come out and discover my presence.

A few minutes later, Cassidy's voice made me look up. Gabe had come out from the back and was behind the counter smiling down at Cassidy with a very. . .friendly sort of smile. Interesting. He hadn't mentioned that he was seeing anyone. Maybe they were just good friends? Cassidy's hand came to rest on his arm while she leaned in to say something quietly. He'd lowered his head to listen and chuckled in reply. His hands came to rest on her hips, and she stretched up to give him a quick peck on the lips before looking around guiltily. *Damn right, little hussy, you're at work,* I thought sharply before pulling myself up short. Where the hell did that come from? It was fine for Gabe to have a girlfriend, of course it was. Why wouldn't it be? It's not like she was competition for me.

Cassidy's guilty scan of the shop caught me watching and snagged on me, causing her to look sharply enough to catch Gabe's attention. He followed her gaze and noticed me. Immediately, he flushed and dropped his hands from her hips as if burned. He said something quickly to her as he walked away from her and out into the shop toward me. "Hey!" he exclaimed, approaching my table. He was still slightly flushed and looked uncomfortable. Even so, he pulled me into an easy hug and turned his face into my hair. "How long have you been here? You could have asked for me. I was just doing inventory." I felt him inhale, smelling my hair. I smiled against his shoulder and gently pulled back to look at him.

"Not long," I shrugged. "I thought I'd surprise you, and I didn't want to interrupt your work. When do you get off?"

He checked his watch. "Supposed to be another hour, but it's been really slow. I can leave now. Have you had lunch?" He reached back to loosen the tie on his apron and started to pull it over his head. "Hey, Cassidy, come here. I want you to meet someone," he called. Cassidy made her way to us warily, looking decidedly hostile. She reached us and put a proprietary hand on Gabe's shoulder.

"I didn't realize you were a friend of Gabe's," she said coolly, holding out her hand only slightly. "I'm Cassidy, Gabe's girlfriend." I shook her hand and smiled indulgently.

"Girlfriend," I said, looking at Gabe, "You naughty boy. When were you going to tell me you had a girlfriend?" I brightened my smile as I looked back at Cassidy. "It's lovely to meet you, Cassidy. I'm Miriam." I withdrew my hand, taking perverse pleasure in watching the little brat's face calculating, wondering who I was to him. Gabe shifted uneasily, looking from Cassidy to me and back again.

"Anyway, I'm going to take off a bit early to grab lunch," Gabe told Cassidy. "I'll see you tonight?" He brushed a kiss on her temple and gave her a one-armed hug. Having packed my laptop away, I straightened, more than ready to leave this weird situation.

"Shall we?" I asked him brightly, taking his customarily proffered arm. Sweet, dorky, gallant boy.

"Yeah, I'm starved," he enthused, Cassidy and the shop all but forgotten as we emerged onto the street. "Wanna go to that Asian burrito fusion place I told you about? It's soooo good."

"Sounds perfect," I grinned, and followed his lead.

Settling back from his chicken tikka burrito in record time, Gabe chuckled smugly. "Told you it was good," he remarked. I nodded in agreement while I chewed. "I'm really glad you came, Miriam. Is this because I made you feel bad about not coming for Family Weekend?" He looked sheepish. I took a deep breath. Time to tell him about Marc. I wiped my mouth and took a sip of diet coke.

"I wanted to see you, of course, because you're my favourite roomie," I teased, "But I also wanted to tell you something sort of cool, and I thought maybe it would be best done in person." He leaned forward eagerly.

"Yeah? Tell me."

"So, that dating app we talking about? And the pictures you took for me? I ended up posting that, after Thanksgiving." Gabe's brow furrowed slightly, but he nodded encouragingly. "I've, um, gotten a few matches, and I, uh, decided to go out on a date with one of them tonight," I finished in a rush. Gabe's mouth opened to speak twice before he responded.

"That's. . .great, Miriam. What do you know about him? You're meeting on neutral ground and everything, right? Where are you meeting him? Did you look him up online to make sure he isn't an axe murderer?" I laughed.

"Whoa, whoa, whoa, kiddo. Slow down," I chuckled. "I read that article about online dating safety you sent me, and I'm following all of the rules," I assured him. "His name is Marc. We haven't exchanged surnames, so I haven't Googled him. I'm meeting him tonight for dinner and drinks at Napolitano's." Gabe considered this information, looking, I guessed, for anything I might have missed. He nodded.

"Okay, well, that seems like a reasonable plan," he allowed finally. "And you know, if anything goes wrong, you just go up to the hostess stand or the bar and let them know you're in trouble. They'll make sure you're safe." His young face looked so concerned. I laughed lightly to relieve the strain.

"I know, kiddo. I read the article. I'll be safe. Don't worry. Can I come to get ready at your place? I'd kind of like to have a shower before I change."

"Yeah, of course. Hey, it's so nice today, why don't we go for a walk around campus and stuff, since I assume you have hours before this dinner thing?"

The day was lovely. Sparkling, and not so cold that we couldn't enjoy some hours of fresh air. By the time we got back to Gabe's room for me to get ready for my date, I was practically giddy with the fresh air, exercise, and time with Gabe. He was also noticeably high on our afternoon. I dropped a kiss on his head before heading into the bathroom to shower.

I discovered that the bathroom door didn't quite latch, so it stood ajar by several inches. Not a big deal, really, since Gabe's roommate was away for the weekend. As I stepped under the water, I heard Gabe's voice greeting someone on the phone. I smiled at the masculine sound of his voice, so grown-up sounding. I showered quickly. I was spoiled by my wonderful rain shower at home. I stepped out and dried myself vigorously. When I lowered the towel, the mirror reflected the view, through the narrow door opening, of Gabe staring intently in my direction. I could not be sure, but I thought he might be watching me. I bit back a mischievous grin. Considering myself in the mirror, I cupped my breasts in my hands, affecting ignorance of my audience. Smoothing my hands down my sides, I turned to examine my ass in the mirror. Not bad, really, for a 40-year-old woman, I thought. *Even if it's a bit weird to be showing your best friend's university-age son your body while he not-so-secretly watches,* grumbled the sniping voice bent on criticizing my recent turn to seductive behaviour with Gabe. A minor crash from the other room brought my attention back to what I could see of it in the mirror.

It was then that I heard the other voice for the first time. A woman's voice. An angry woman, by the sound of it. "Are you even listening to me?" the woman demanded. "Gabe! God damn it. I asked if you were listening to me." I heard Gabe murmur something mildly. Better get dressed and get out there in case he needed moral support or something. I ducked behind the door to slip into bra and panties before pulling my cute little date dress over my head. I zipped as much as I could and padded my way out to the other room. "Hey Gabe, can you zip me, please?" I asked as I entered the room, pretending I didn't know I was awkwardly blundering into an argument.

Gabe looked amused at my entry. Cassidy - it was Cassidy who was angrily charging Gabe with not paying attention – turned blazing eyes on me. "Interesting, Gabe, that you did not mention you had a woman in the shower when I got here," she commented dryly. "Is that Helmut Lang? Who wears a designer dress to go on a Friday night date?" she demanded with a sneer. "Are you some kind of high-priced escort or something?" Her head started nodding, as if she had solved a puzzle, so she didn't immediately notice the effect her question had had on Gabe. "That's it, isn't it?

You're a gold-digging call-girl after his family's money." Gabe's expression darkened, and he seemed to grow several inches as he stood.

"Get out," he said, very quietly to Cassidy. She crossed her arms defiantly, looking from one of us to the other, making no move to leave.

"I'm not going anywhere until you tell me what the fuck is going on, Gabe. Otherwise, we're done," Cassidy retorted. Gabe closed the distance between us and zipped my dress the rest of the way. He stood next to me, half a step in front of me, like he was shielding me.

Voice shaking, but not raised, Gabe repeated, "Get. Out. Cassidy. You have forfeited your right to an explanation of anything. Just go." I felt sorry for her, in a way. She looked angry, but also hurt and confused. And of course, she thought I was the woman who was fucking her boyfriend, when in reality, I was, well, sort of the woman fucking her boyfriend, but slightly more complicated. Finally, her shoulders slumped in defeat, and she grabbed her bag to go. She stopped in front of me and treated me to a slow, disgusted head-to-toe appraisal.

"Don't think you can start charging him once you get him hooked," she spit it out nastily. "His family has money because his mom is some bestselling pulp author, but he doesn't have any, and I doubt she'll want to fund his whoring." I'd been feeling generous. I had. But the dig at Sasha's writing was too much. I brushed an imaginary fleck of lint from my bare shoulder.

"I think Gabe was just ready for a woman," I said in a bored tone. "He told me he was getting tired of melodramatic little girls." Cassidy flounced out the door, slamming it behind her. We were silent for several seconds before Gabe started chuckling. The chuckle quickly became a full-blown laugh. I couldn't help but join him.

"I was ready to kick her out for calling you a whore, and you didn't get mad until she insulted my mom's writing," he gasped between laughs. "She called you a call girl, and you didn't bat an eyelash. But she insulted my mom and writing, and the claws came out. She's lucky she left when she did!" I couldn't deny it. Maybe a 19-20-year-old girl saw it differently, but, at 40, calling me a whore just wasn't nearly as big a deal to me as it was belittling my best friend and my career in one breath.

I put on my makeup in the bathroom, with Gabe perched on the vanity, watching me and keeping me company. We talked and laughed easily while I got ready. Finally, all dolled up, I headed downstairs to get a car to take me to the restaurant. It wasn't far, but the Louboutins I had chosen for the evening, which looked fabulous, were completely unsuited for walking even a couple of blocks.

When I walked in, my eye sought and found the only lone man in the dining room. In confirmation of my suspicion that this was Marc, the maître d' showed me to the table near the window, where a tall, handsome man sat alone. He stood as we approached the table. "Ah, Miriam," he greeted, turning the hand I offered him to shake and kissing it, instead. He held my hand a moment longer and looked at me intensely. "It is simply wonderful," he said rather superciliously, "To have this opportunity to meet you." He indicated my seat and pushed it in as I sat, before resuming his seat.

"Yes, it's, um, nice to meet you, too, Marc," I responded, suddenly nervous. I was overwhelmed by the sense that this had been a terrible mistake. I shouldn't be here. I didn't want to be here. Part of me wanted to deliver a hasty excuse and leave immediately to go find Gabe and spend the evening with him instead. That's what I wanted to be doing. Not having dinner with this self-impressed stranger. But the social urge to be polite won out. I heaved an internal sigh and determined to make the best of it. After all, I didn't need to go home with him, and I didn't need to ever see him again if I didn't want to. Resolution reached, I tried to focus on enjoying myself as much as possible.

Dinner was superb. I made mental notes of everything we had, to tell Gabe about it later. Throughout the meal, Marc kept up a steady conversation, balancing things about himself with questions about me adroitly. I discovered that he had read some of my books. We also learned that we both loved the opera, preferred the mountains to the beach, and secretly enjoyed karaoke. All in all, Marc was very pleasant and easy to talk to. It should have been exciting. Instead, I had a growing dread about the end of the meal. For dessert, we ordered a piece of chocolate torte to share, but after one bite, I set my fork down. I didn't want to share it with this man. I wanted to get it in a box and go find Gabe to share it with him. Marc finished the torte without comment, probably assuming I was on a diet.

After dinner, we exited the restaurant and walked slowly toward Downtown, enjoying the night air. "May I interest you in a drink at my place?" he asked, stopping and wrapping both arms around me with a little too much confidence. "I could show you those photographs I mentioned, from the hiking trip." He lowered his head to place a kiss at my temple, and lingered, clearly wanting to go further. This was what I had planned, really. I was going to go out with Marc, fuck him to get this energy out of my system, and stop having lustful urges toward my best friend's son. Straightforward, easy, and going exactly according to plan so far. And I had no desire to go through with it. I searched for a graceful exit.

"Oh, that's very kind, Marc, but I have this writing deadline I'm up against, so I really should take a raincheck for that," I ventured. In an instant, his jovial flirtation was gone, replaced by a hard, sullen expression. He raised his head and started to shake it, laughing bitterly.

"You bitches are all alike, aren't you?" Marc began. "You can guzzle my wine and order without looking at the prices. You can pretend you like opera and Virginia Woolf. But once the bill is paid and I want my dick sucked, you've got to go because you have an early morning." By this point, we had reached the end of the block. I increased my pace, planning to walk straight to my car without saying a word and driving away, but Marc grabbed my arm sharply and spun me to face him, almost making me lose my balance in the process. With his other hand, he made a fist in my hair, holding me in place while he smashed his mouth against mine. I struggled and managed to break his grasp.

"You fucking asshole," I shrieked. "What the fuck is wrong with you?" I turned back toward the restaurant and fled, heedless for the moment of my unfortunate footwear.

"Don't you run away from me, Miriam," Marc yelled, giving chase. "You owe me this, you frigid bitch!" He got hold of my wrap and would have pulled me back with it, but I shrugged out of it, sacrificing it to the cause of getting away. He cursed, but my release of the garment had caught him by surprise. Fuelled by fear and anger, I was able to get enough head start that if I screamed, I could probably get help. I didn't hear Marc behind me anymore, but I didn't slow to find out where he was. I ran all the way back to the restaurant and headed straight for the ladies' room, locking the door behind me. I paused to catch my breath for just a second.

Hands shaking slightly, I leaned against the bathroom wall and pulled my phone out to text Gabe. *Hey, kiddo, where are you?*

The Read indicator turned blue almost instantly.

Miriam? Are you okay? Did something happen? Do you need me to come to get you somewhere? I'm with some friends at Baron's. That pizza place right near Napolitano's. The dots danced a couple of times, but he didn't say anything further.

No, no, it's okay. Plan just fell through. Would it be okay if I joined you, do you think? Would your friends mind? I hated to interrupt his night out with his friends, but at least he wasn't out on a date, and I didn't want to drive home to an empty house just yet after the experience with Marc.

Of course. Should I come to get you? He replied immediately. I pictured his forehead bunched in a scowl of worry and concentration.

I'll be there in a minute. It's fine, kiddo, I promise. I put my phone back in my purse and peered into the mirror over the sink. My lipstick had gotten smudged, but the waterproof mascara had lived up to its promises, so I didn't have raccoon eyes, at least. I fixed my lipstick and put my hair up into a messy bun to hide the dishevelment from Marc's aggressive advances before heading out the door for Baron's before Gabe got worried and called out a search party.

He was pacing out front as I approached, peering up the street, watching for me. When he saw me, his shoulders relaxed, and he hurried toward me. "Mir? Are you okay? Are you sure?" He searched my face as he ran his hands over my shoulders and down my arms, as if checking for wounds. I shivered. "Shit, Miriam, why don't you have a jacket on? You must be freezing in that cute little dress," he admonished, unzipping his hoodie and removing it against my protestations.

"No, really, Gabe, I'm fine. Plans just fell through. And I left my jacket in the car. That's my fault. No need for you to be cold." My protests were useless, since the sweet boy was draping the hoodie over my shoulders before pushing my arms gently through the sleeves, even as I protested. Admittedly, I was both warmer and greatly comforted, cocooned in the warmth from Gabe's body and his familiar scent. Fine, if it would make him happy, I would wear it. He fumbled to engage the zipper at the bottom and started to zip it up, taking care not to catch the delicate material of my dress in the zipper. I watched his hands, strong and sure, intent on taking care of me. When the zipper reached the level of my breasts, which were pretty generously displayed by the low-cut dress, he slowed, unconsciously taking a deep breath and holding it. I looked at his face when he stopped, and waited, mesmerized by his expression. After a few seconds, he released the breath and resumed, zipping the hoodie to the top and raising his eyes to meet mine for a long second.

"Do you want to go home?" he asked. "I could take you home now, and you could drive me back in the morning."

"No, it's already kind of late for that, and I don't want to interrupt your night. I also. . .could kind of go for a drink, if you're sure your friends won't mind," I said uncertainly.

"They won't," he responded decisively. He took my arm and opened the door to usher me in. A folk duo was on a small stage at the back wall, currently covering Simon & Garfunkel's "Scarborough Fair," as Gabe guided me to a table of people in the corner. Everyone looked up as we approached the table. "Hey, guys, this is-" he started. Shit. I didn't want him to be embarrassed by his mom's friend showing up at the bar on a Friday night. I knew he didn't see it that way, but still.

"I'm Miriam," I interrupted, waving at the group and smiling brightly. "And this guy," I squeezed his arm and gave him a peck on the cheek, "Just rescued me from a rather unpleasant blind date."

"You said you wanted a drink? If you want alcohol, you'll have to get it, because they card here, but they have root beer and stuff. What would you like?" he asked.

"Hmm," I considered. "You know what I like, Gabe. A root beer sounds good. I haven't had one in ages." He chuckled.

"Yeah, it's been ages for me too. Ok, I'll go grab us a couple." He dropped a kiss on the top of my head and headed for the bar. A tall, lanky boy with a mop of curls had brought another chair over and set it next to the empty chair I assumed was Gabe's.

"Thanks," I said, gratefully sinking into the seat. My feet were killing me just from the limited walking I had done in these heels. Gabe returned with two root beers and handed me one. "Slánte," I said, holding up my bottle to his.

"Slánte," he confirmed, clinking his bottle against mine. The mop-headed boy exchanged an amused look with the girl next to him.

"Thanks for letting me crash your night," I remarked, striving to sound nonchalant. "I-I wasn't ready to go home alone just yet." Mop-head made a sympathetic noise.

"A friend of Gabe's is always welcome. Especially if it isn't Cassidy," was one girl's only answer. My face must have shown my confusion.

"Cassidy isn't super popular around here," explained the other girl. "She's possessive and just," she shrugged. "She isn't super popular around here," she reiterated simply in conclusion. I glanced at Gabe to gauge his reaction. He was taking a drink of root beer and looking unconcerned and uninterested. No further mention was made of Cassidy.

Talk was easy – mostly I talked with Gabe and listened to the others talking about school and exams coming up. I went up sheepishly to get a pitcher of beer, since my "date" wasn't able to, and assured the bartender it was for me, following a scary ending to a blind date. She made sympathetic noises, even as she handed me enough glasses for the table.

Chapter 11

Leaving the bar a while later, we decided to walk the short distance to the dorm. We set a leisurely pace, my arm tucked in Gabe's. We walked at least a full block in comfortable silence before he spoke, "So are you going to tell me what really happened?" he asked quietly.

"What do you mean, 'what really happened'?" I responded, mind racing. Gabe sighed.

"Look, Miriam, you don't have to tell me if you don't want to, but I know you. Something happened. This wasn't some neutral 'plans falling through' thing." I sighed, smiling fondly.

"Yeah, okay. I don't know why I thought I was going to get away with not telling you in the first place," I laughed softly. "You know me awfully well." He grunted in response.

"Too right. Just tell me," he stopped and gently turned me to face him. "Did he hurt you, or. . .anything like that?" He was upset, imagining what might have happened, trying to keep his composure. I reached up to stroke his face.

"I'm fine, Gabe. Yes, he got a little. . .aggressive. I thought I wanted, um, a physical encounter. But when he invited me to come over, it just wasn't-it wasn't what I wanted. I declined, and he got angry, called me, um, called me a name. Then he kind of grabbed me," I paused to gulp some deep breaths, struggling not to cry. "Grabbed me and pulled my hair and, um, kissed me. . .I ran back to the restaurant. In these," I indicated my heels and winced. "I went straight to the bathroom, in case he followed, and texted you, because-" I stopped again, breathing deeply and swiping angrily at tears. He cupped my chin gently and tipped my head up to look at him.

"Because what, Miriam?" he asked, trying so hard to maintain his calm, for my sake.

"Because the only thing I wanted- what I needed, was just to see you," I finished, unable to suppress a sob. He pulled me into his arms, holding me tightly and cradling the back of my head with one hand. I felt a growl in his chest.

"Fucking bastard," he hissed, through clenched teeth. "Sick, fucking, piece of shit bastard." He was trembling with anger. "I shouldn't have taken those sexy pictures of you, letting these disgusting fucks see how gorgeous and sexy you are." He buried his face in my hair and I heard the angry tears in his voice. "I'm sorry, Mir. I'm sorry I wasn't there to protect you and kick this guy's fucking ass." He looked down at me, his face a rictus of misery. My heart ached for him. I lifted my hands to cup his face, gently kissed each cheek, and then each eyelid, and the tip of his nose. He brought his forehead to rest against mine, both of us breathing hard through a welter of conflicting emotions. Finally, he pressed a lingering kiss on the top of my head, and put an arm around my shoulders, reaching behind himself to grab my hand and pull it around to rest around his waist. "Come on. Let's go to my room, get your poor feet out of those heels, and get some rest." He gave a sardonic laugh. "I'll plan how I'm going to find this guy and kick his ass tomorrow. Deal?" He looked down at me, flashing me a boyish grin.

"Deal," I agreed and followed his lead toward his building. Back in Gabe's room, at last, I gratefully kicked off my heels. "I think I may burn those tomorrow," I laughed. "I never want to see them again."

I took a seat on his bed, and he sat on the floor, back against his roommate's bed, facing me. I spotted the stack of catalogues I had teasingly handed over with such wicked glee earlier today. It felt like so much longer. I smiled sadly. "You know, I was so convinced this," I waved my hands down at myself vaguely, "Dating thing was going to go well, I bought one of the sets from in there to wear for it," I confessed, indicated the catalogues. Gabe gaped at me wordlessly. "Surprised?" I asked laughingly.

"When you say, 'from in there,'" he clarified. "You mean, like. . ." he trailed off, unequal to finishing the thought. I giggled mischievously.

"Uh-huh," I confirmed. "I judged by the, uh, wear of the pages, and picked one that seemed to be a favourite, figuring if you thought it was sexy in the catalogue, probably Ma- er, my date, would agree." There was a heavy silence before Gabe cleared his throat.

"Whi-which one?" he choked out, breathing shallow. I leaned down and flipped through until I found the catalogue I was thinking of.

"It was in here. Page 6 or 7, I think? It seemed to be one you really liked." Hand shaking slightly, Gabe turned the pages almost reverently before coming to the indicated page. A small squeak escaped him. I peered down at the page he was looking at.

"Yup, that one, the black one," I told him. He made a noise in the back of his throat. I grinned saucily. "Wanna see?" I asked. He gazed at me wordlessly and nodded. I hesitated only briefly, and then took a deep breath, sitting up. Holding his gaze, I slowly unzipped the hoodie I was still wearing, revealing the dress again. I shrugged my way out of first one strap, and then the other, lowering the dress enough to reveal the bra. Eyes still on his face, I lifted my hips off the bed enough to push the dress up to reveal black satin panties with lace trim to match the bra. As if in a trance, Gabe crawled toward his bed from his place in front of the other bed. "Mmm, yes, I can see now why the crawling is so hot," I murmured. He stopped in front of me, his eyes wide, his breathing shallow.

He gripped my hips and pulled me closer to the edge of the bed, wedging himself between my legs as he shifted me. Slowly, one hand moved to unbuckle his belt. My breathing grew shallow. Gabe popped the button of his jeans and eased the zipper down. I could see his cock straining to get out. His hand disappeared from sight, taking his cock in his fist behind the concealment of his boxer briefs. "Yeah, Miriam, that-" he said, his breathing threadbare. "That was always my favourite." His eyes on my breasts, traveling down to examine the matching panties, was so intense, it was like a caress.

I let my hands come up to cup my breasts, drawing his gaze back upward. Already puckering, my nipples hardened between my pinched fingers, sharply outlined by the thin cloth covering them. Gabe arched his pelvis slightly into his hand in response, emitting a low moan. I took hold of the bottom of my dress, bunched at my waist to expose the panties, and drew it up, slowly, to bring the dress over my head. I carelessly let the dress fall to the bed, attention rapt on Gabe's response. After returning my hands to my breasts, I let them roam, smoothing them down over my stomach, sending anticipatory zings of excitement further down, between my legs.

My fingers found the tiny silver key attached to the bow at the centre of the panties' waistband and toyed with it idly. Gabe groaned. Past the key, I find the satin covering my pussy damp. In the back of my mind, a voice objected, *Wet for Gabe, Miriam. Wet for Sasha's son, who's less than half your age. This isn't right.* I looked at Gabe, at his sweet, young face, looking at me with such affection and trust in his eyes. *What's wrong with it, really, though?* I asked my judgmental critic. I shook my head slightly to dismiss the voice, consigning it to the closet where I sent shame to sit alone and reconsider its position. *Later, not now. Now, I want this.* I stroked my fingers up and down several times, biting my lip, feeling myself grow wetter under the strokes.

"Let me see, Gabe. Let me watch you," I gasped. I tugged the panties to the side, exposing my soaking flesh to the air of the room. . .and Gabe's piercing gaze. I ran a finger lightly along my sensitized slit, panting now. "Please, kiddo. I want to see," I pleaded. Hesitantly, Gabe used his free hand to push his jeans and boxer briefs down to reveal his cock in the other hand. I had seen some of it during my accidental Peeping Miriam session before Thanksgiving, and of course, I'd felt him each morning of that week at my back, but seeing him in all his adult glory, now, on the floor before me, was a different matter altogether. I couldn't hold in a moan of longing.

Gabe's answering, "Miriam!" was a mixture of matched longing and confusion. I slid one finger, and then two, into myself, my body clenching on them instinctively. I saw the gleam of pre-come appear on the head of Gabe's cock and ached to taste it, but didn't dare break the spell by pushing for more. Instead, I increased my speed, fucking myself rapidly and hard now, wishing for a toy to make the task easier and more satisfying. My head back, my breath coming in sobs, I felt my climax building and chased it feverishly.

Tentative fingers on my thigh brought my eyes open sharply. Gabe's hand was high on my thigh, and he looked at me in a silent request for permission. Swallowing hard against a suddenly very dry mouth, I nodded mutely.

He lowered his face between my legs, pressing his lips against my mound with only the thin satin between us. He inhaled deeply before opening his mouth and extending his tongue to run down my slit, the dampness from his tongue mingling with my moisture to render the satin hot and damp. I moaned and opened my legs to him further. He braced his hands on my thighs, massaging the insides of them high up with his thumbs, licking me several more times through the panties before hooking his thumbs on the sides of the panties and looking up at me, tugging gently. I lifted my hips enough to allow him to pull the panties from under my ass and ease them slowly down my legs, planting hot kisses along my thighs as he did. My breath ragged, I buried my fingers in his hair, not guiding his head, yet, but needing to feel him under my fingers. Having slipped my panties down and over my feet to lie on the floor next to the catalogues, he kissed his way up the inside of the other leg, finally taking my ass in his hands and pulling me into his face. His tongue flat, he used it to lick along the length of my slit before taking the swollen bud of my clit into his mouth and suckling it. I gathered handfuls of the bedspread in my fists, head thrown back, panting hard. "Gabe," I breathed. Relentlessly, he licked and suckled me, holding me still as I writhed in his grasp, chasing my pleasure, moaning his name like a prayer. "Please, Gabe, oh fuck, I want to, oh please don't stop," I cried desperately, fingers laced in his hair and tugging harder as my climax began to build. His shuddering breaths against my damp and sensitive flesh felt like the breath of life itself, raising goosebumps all over and driving me mad. I felt myself about to fall and was powerless to resist or move closer, given over completely to his playing upon my body. Then I was falling, crying out, rocked by wave after wave of earth-shifting sensation. Gabe crawled onto the bed and held me tenderly as I trembled, his hand stroking featherlight between my legs as I came back to myself. He was still mostly dressed, his erection jutting up over his lowered jeans, but seemed content to let me enjoy my aftershocks.

I stroked him, hungry for him, needing to give him something akin to the gift he had bestowed upon me. Before pulling them off, I looked to him for permission. "Fuck, yes, please," he begged in response. I pulled his jeans down and off, tossing them to the floor. I giggled and pulled his socks off and tossed them aside. Watching his eyes, I crawled up his body, predatory. His breathing came in gasps as I paused to nip and suck at his legs on my way up. I drank in the sight of his straining erection, glistening at the tip.

I reached up to pull the hair tie out, releasing my messy bun so my hair came down around my shoulders in wavy cascades. Running my lips along the inside of one of his thighs, I massaged the other with my hand through a curtain of hair. Gabe's hips came off the bed in an eager thrust. Moving higher, I wrapped a thick swath of my hair around the base of his cock, squeezing him in my fist as I daintily licked the droplet of moisture from the eye of his cock. "Mmmm," I hummed in satisfaction. I took the tip into my mouth, making my lips a rigid O constricting around it, swirling my tongue around him inside my mouth. My efforts were rewarded with a long, low moan of sweet torment from this beautiful boy. "Miriam," he begged. "Please."

I lowered my head gradually, taking him further into my mouth, bit by bit. I moved my hair grip to wrap it around his balls, leaving me fuller access to the whole of his shaft, and allowing me to massage his balls gently through the medium of that contrasting texture. I felt one hand tentatively cup my head, applying slight pressure. I reached back with one hand, laying it over his and applying additional pressure, letting him know it was fine for him to push my head down. Once assured of my approval, he pressed harder, helping me to go down harder, taking him hard against the back of my throat. I moaned deep in my throat, causing my throat to constrict and vibrate against his sensitive tip. I hollowed my cheeks to create suction and began to move more quickly, up and down, on his cock, sucking and taking him as deep as possible each time.

I tasted the tell-tale saltiness of more pre-come and knew he was close. I dug my fingers into his ass and redoubled my efforts, fucking him with my mouth with total abandon. His gasps and wordless moans tracked his progress. Close, so close, closer. Just when I knew he was about to explode into my mouth, he pushed me off his cock and rolled me onto my back, so that when the explosion came, he spent on my chest and stomach, some of it on the bra he had admired so much for so long, but most of it, stark white on my flesh.

His look, as he lay on his side, propped up on one elbow, was one of astonishment. He considered the come he'd spilled on me before reaching out a finger and drawing it through the cooling spill. Absently, he traced a heart with this new fingerpaint. He caught me watching him and ducked his head, embarrassed. "Oh, sorry," he said suddenly, reaching onto the floor for his discarded shirt, making to wipe me clean with it. I stopped him.

"Kiddo, wait," I stopped him. Holding his gaze, I ran my fingers down his arm, down his hand, to the tips of his fingers where they rested on my abdomen. I took hold of the finger that had drawn the heart, still damp at the tip. I guided his fingertip through the heart, playfully adding an arrow. Then I lifted his finger to my mouth to suck it clean, reminding me of that first night of Thanksgiving break, and the ganache I licked off my finger, creating that hungry electricity between us. When I'd finished, he used the shirt to gently wipe me clean. Hesitatingly, he kissed me softly. I returned his kiss before nestling myself tightly against him. My head rested on his chest, one hand resting over his heart. He hummed contentedly at almost the same time as I, bringing his arms around me. "Gabe?" I murmured sleepily.

"Yeah, Miriam?" he mumbled, after a pause.

"I'm glad I'm here, Gabe."

"I'm glad you're here, too, Miriam," he answered, kissing my head and inhaling deeply. Then we slept.

Coming awake, I was initially confused. The light in the room was unfamiliar, and the bed was definitely unfamiliar. The body I was curled around, fortunately, was not unfamiliar. Without opening my eyes, I knew from his scent and the feel of his arms around me that I was with Gabe. I snuggled against him, rubbing my face against his chest, marvelling at what had happened and wondering vaguely if I should be upset about it.

"Mir? You awake?" he asked.

"Mmhmm, I'm awake, kiddo."

"Miriam, we gotta get up," he replied, causing me to sit up and look at him in concern. He grinned sheepishly. "I'm starving," he explained. My surprised laugh quickly devolved into both of us cackling like hyenas.

"Okay," I gasped finally, "But I have to have a quick shower before we go out." I showered and dried quickly, wrapping my hair up in a towel turban. I considered my options before settling on wearing one of Gabe's t-shirts over my dress from the night before, tying a knot at the back to make it less baggy. Hair in a damp bun and hoodie zipped up over my unconventional ensemble, the only remaining problem was my shoes, but there was nothing to be done there. I shrugged mentally.

Gabe got in the shower after me, and I took the time to jot down a few notes for my book. I'd had an idea when I was falling asleep for how the queen would convince her young husband that it didn't matter so much what people said about them. It was going to be a pretty good speech. Gabe got out of the shower just as I was finishing and got dressed before we went downstairs in search of breakfast. We went across the street to his favourite crepe shop. Halfway through breakfast, a shadow fell across the table. Mop-head and the brunette girl, whom I had met at Baron's the night before, were standing over our table, grinning. Mop-head – I learned finally that his name was Matthew – allowed himself a leisurely appraisal of my damp hair and morning after outfit before turning a

107

congratulatory expression to Gabe. "Having a little breakfast, huh?" he chortled. "Excellent choice. . .of place. They make great food here." I ducked my head to hide a grin. Gabe was blushing but maintained his composure. The brunette – Lisette – cleared her throat and tugged at Matthew's arm.

"I'm sure they don't want our company this morning, babe," said Lisette pointedly. "Miriam, I hope we'll be seeing you again soon," she said to me. She gave Gabe an approving nod, and dragged Matthew away, leaving us both blushing wordlessly.

After they left, we finished our breakfasts and emerged onto the street contemplating our next moves. "You know," he commented, "The rest of that stuff you needed at the library, we could get it done faster if we worked together. We should be able to knock out the rest of the list in an hour, working together." I looked down out at my unorthodox outfit.

"Gabe," I started, patiently. He held up a hand with mock severity.

"None of that, Miriam," he said with a wolfish grin. "You'll fit right in with the Saturday-morning grad student crowd. Everyone will just think I'm dating my sexy TA." He pulled me to him without reservation and kissed me as if we really were a normal couple. When he lifted his head, we looked at each other in confusion for a few moments before he shrugged and took my hand. "Not borrowing trouble," he said with finality, and led me in the direction of the library.

After scanning the final journal articles, Gabe took my hand and led me to the stairwell. "I want to show you something," he said, pulling me along. We went up a floor and wove our way through a labyrinth of stacks before we came to a stop at a shelf that looked just like the others. "Here," he said, with satisfaction. I looked in bewilderment at the shelf he indicated, and then I saw. It was my books. He had taken me to where the books I'd already published were, and he had done so without consulting signage even once. He knew the way. Standing behind me, he put his arms around my waist and rested his chin on my shoulder. "You don't know how often I have come here," he whispered. "Just to be close to you."

I leaned back against him, surprised and excited to feel him hard against my ass. Pressing into him, I craned my head up to look at him wonderingly. "Really? That's. . .thank you," I said quietly, overwhelmed. He bent to nibble my ear.

"I'm your biggest fan," he murmured, "Since you told me bedtime stories about queens and kings and ghosts and vampires. Your stories were even better than my mom's. Just don't ever tell her I said that!" He chuckled. I searched his eyes, trying to understand this new set of dynamics. He looked into my eyes, expression hooded, before bowing his head to bury his face in my hair. "Miriam?" he breathed, part question, part appeal.

I leaned back into him more heavily, loving the feeling of him breathing in my hair. One of his hands went up under the hoodie I was wearing to take hold of a breast. The other worked at bunching my dress, inching it up and up until he was able to work his way under it. His fingers brushed me and stilled. Gabe growled deep in his chest, "Miriam," he said severely, nipping my ear. "You are not wearing panties." I giggled softly.

"I didn't have any to change into," I answered simply. "If you recall," I added saucily, "The ones I was wearing last night got pretty dirty." In response, he reached in and playfully pinched my clit, drawing a sharp gasp from me. Gabe brought the hand that had been holding one breast to put it firmly against my mouth.

"No noise, Miriam," he said in a tone at once filthy and playful. "If you want me to fuck you with my fingers right here in the library, you have to be completely quiet, okay?" I breathed unevenly, aching for him to touch me more, harder. He pinched me again. "Okay, Mir? You have to agree," he insisted. I nodded quickly. Anything. I would agree to anything right now, to get Gabe to touch me there in the library aisle where he had been visiting my books to be close to me. In this strange new space, the sweetness of his visiting my books mingled with a new sense, a lover's sense, heating my skin and filling me with a need for him. Him. Gabe. My best friend's son, the child I'd watched grow up, had become a man, and I needed more of him.

Having secured my agreement, he pushed into me, pushing me against the bookshelves, his hand firmly between my legs, stroking my wet slit. "You're so wet," he exclaimed into my hair. "That's so hot, your sexy little pussy all ready for me," he growled, using one finger to probe into my folds, exploring me, spreading my fluids, making me more inflamed with every movement. Behind his hand, I whimpered with need, desperate for more. "You want a finger inside you, Miriam?" He demanded quietly against my ear. I nodded vigorously, making him chuckle. "So needy," he chided, pushing not one, but two fingers deep into me. I would have cried out if his hand hadn't been over my mouth. "Is that what you want, needy lady?" he teased. "Is that enough? Should I stop now?" The brat was practically chortling, showing no respect for the fact that I would very probably die if he didn't give me an orgasm soon. I was writhing against him, desperate for release. He bit my ear again, harder this time, increasing the pace of his fingers, blessedly. I dug my fingers into his forearms, consciously fighting the urge to scream as waves of pleasure overtook me.

With the evidence of my release dripping down my leg, I turned in Gabe's arms and kissed him greedily. I pressed a hand against his throbbing erection through his jeans. His hand, tangled in my hair, tightened to a fist, and he groaned. I gave him a devilish look, licked my lips, and started to drop to my knees. "Here? But M-" he started, but I cut him off, looking around before taking him by the hand and leading him to a study carrel nearby. I dropped to my knees and crawled under the desk, looking saucily over my shoulder at him before turning to beckon him to sit. He looked around nervously but gave me a devastating grin and sat. I pulled his chair in further, angling it as much away from the stacks as possible. I eagerly reached for his zipper again, pausing to attain his permission. He looked excited, but uncertain, still craning to see if anyone was nearby.

"No one can see me under here, kiddo. You just probably shouldn't, um, yell or anything," I said, giggling. He looked down at me, burying his hands in my hair and bending way down to kiss me.

"You," he whispered, "Are very naughty, and if you get me expelled from school, I am never going to let you forget it." He chuckled, that sexy, arrogant chuckle he'd developed that made me go weak in the knees every time. Then he sat back, waiting for me to make my move. I grinned and licked my lips, reaching for his zipper and lowering it, my eyes never leaving his. I reached in and freed him. He was hard, ready for me. For a moment, I considered what else I'd like to do, considered climbing onto his lap, but it was too soon. With one last look in his eyes, I lowered my head to swirl my tongue around him, enjoying the satin softness stretched over his jutting cock. I licked him from tip to base, following the line of his vein. I licked his length all around him, from tip to base, base to tip, and back. I took him in my mouth, delighted by how difficult it was to take him all at once.

His fingers, in my hair, tightened when he hit the back of my throat, fisting hard when I pressed on, opening my throat to accommodate him. I sucked on him as I lifted my head away, until only the tip was still in my mouth. Gently, at first, he pushed me back down, hips leaving his chair slightly to push his way back into me. I hummed

112

contentedly deep in my throat, earning me a convulsive thrust of his hips. "Fuck, that hum when I'm that deep," he whisper-moaned. "So good, Miriam, do it again." I did, loving the feeling of his body going rigid in response. Faster now, he gave little thrusts, fucking my throat from his seat. "Miriam," he gasped. His hands gripped me, held me in place, while he thrust deeply, once, twice, and a third time, staying there, perfectly still, while his seed pumped into my throat. I could hear that he was struggling not to cry out, though by now, anyone in earshot had heard enough to know what was going on in this corner. He trembled as he gradually softened and relaxed.

He pushed his chair back and pulled me out from under the desk. He hauled me into his arms, so I was half-standing, half-perched on his lap. He buried his face in my neck, tears dampening my hair. I wrapped my arms around his shoulders and held him. Finally, he pulled away to look in my face. "What are we doing, Miriam?" He seemed to search my face for answers. Brushing a strand of hair out my face, he went on. "You're gorgeous. You're sexy. You're. . ." He gave a frustrated huff. "My friends thought we were a couple. It just seemed obvious to them. What does that mean? You're my mom's best friend. Way too old for me. My parents would shit. I don't care how old you are, but shouldn't the rest of it be apparent, somehow? That we aren't allowed to be together? Why don't they see that? Why don't we?" The tears were streaming down his face unchecked.

He was quiet long enough that I realized he was waiting for some answer. I didn't have much of one, but I had to try. I reached to wipe away his tears. "Maybe nothing is wrong with us," I ventured. I held up a hand to forestall his protest. "Why does something have to be? I know society has rules, and in those terms, yes, we're already probably freaks. But what if those rules . . .aren't so universal? What if they aren't for us? I've been reading and writing about people loving people and fucking people in every conglomeration for years. What if that was all to prepare for this? Prepare us to be different?" He looked down at our twined hands, turning them one way, and then another, studying them. When he looked back at my face, his expression was filled with so much affection, it took my breath away. This beautiful, magic boy. I kissed his forehead, his cheeks, his nose, and finally, quickly, his lips. "I'm going to go home, kiddo. I have work to do, and we both have some things to think about. I'll see you at Christmas break in a couple weeks." I disentangled myself from his embrace. "I-I'll talk to you soon, Gabe."

"I'll talk to you soon, Miriam." I walked away, legs a little shaky, down the stairs and across the street to where I'd left my car. I got into the car and got the door closed behind me just as the tears started. Now that I didn't need to be strong for Gabe, my own fear and confusion overwhelmed me. Was I right, that maybe there was nothing wrong with us? Even if I was, what if we didn't want to follow the same path? Was one of us destined to break the other's heart? For that matter, if that happened, wouldn't it break both our hearts? Taking some deep breaths, I squared my shoulders. Regardless, I had work to do. Time to go home and write about someone else's unconventional romantic entanglements and give my own a rest. I chuckled at the self-deprecation there. *"Life,"* I thought, as I merged onto the freeway toward home, *"is complicated."*

Chapter 12

The morning they planned to try to break the curse, the queen woke to find her husband sitting at the window looking pensive. She rose and went to him, allowing him to fold her into his arms. "What troubles you, husband?" His answer was slow in coming.

"I've just been thinking. After today, the nature of our marriage will no longer be a matter of conjecture. Everyone will have confirmation that we- that ours is a true marriage. I worry about what they'll say. I worry about whether-" his voice trailed off.

Jacqueline fought the hurt his comments had caused and pulled back from his embrace. "I see. You're regretting the marriage. I thought you would, before, but by now, I thought perhaps-" She started to turn, planning to go to her dressing room for a good, angry weep before summoning Mathilde to help her prepare for the day. Eduard caught her arm and hurried around to stand in front of her, dropping to his knees to hug her legs.

"No," he said with real anguish. "No, my love, you misunderstand." He looked up at her from his supplicant position. "I worry that we will be bombarded, that you, especially, will be bombarded, with insults. That we will never have peace. That you will be unhappy and regret. . .well, regret me. I don't know how to prepare for it, how to protect you." He chuckled at his own impotence. "The mostly highly-ranked man in the kingdom, and

116

I can't protect my wife from her enemies. What sort of man am I?"

Jacqueline sank to her knees in relief, joining her husband and peppering his face with kisses. "Eduard, it doesn't matter. Those rules, those universal rules about men and women and marriage – all of that. Those rules aren't as universal as people believe." She paused to kiss him thoroughly. "It isn't normal for a woman my age to marry a man your age. I have no use for normal. We have our magic that brought us together, our magic that binds us, and the magic between us that has allowed us to love each other. Why would we want normal, when we have magic?"

Eduard considered the queen's point only briefly before standing and pulling her to her feet. He picked her up tenderly and carried her to the bed, where he made love to her in celebration of the truth of her words. Afterward, she dozed in his arms while he watched her, memorizing every feature. He was terrified of what they planned to try that afternoon, but she thought it would work, so he would go along. Nonetheless, he did not plan to take his eyes from her for a moment before then, drinking in her presence, both for strength, and in case things went wrong.

Late in the afternoon, the sovereigns and their entourage arrived at the site. No life of any kind was in evidence. A general sense of dread and sorrow worried at the consciousness of all assembled. Jacqueline and Eduard surveyed the bleak landscape before exchanging a long look.

"The theory is good, my love," Eduard reassured the queen. "This will work. And if it doesn't-"

"If it doesn't," agreed the queen, "We will try something else." Neither mentioned the possibility that failure might preclude the possibility of trying anything else later.

Eduard stepped down from the carriage and waved away the footmen who moved forward to help his wife alight, preferring to do so himself. On this occasion, it seemed important that no one touch her other than himself. When she offered him her hand, Jacqueline could feel that he was already reaching for the magic, spooling what he was able to find, just as she was, though it was far thinner here than they were accustomed to drawing on in the capital.

"Will we be able to spool enough, do you think?" Eduard asked his wife quietly.

"We will see that it is enough," Jacqueline responded, squeezing his hand. "Fortunately, as we've discovered, our union," her uncharacteristically shy smile at this was so fleeting, only Eduard saw it, "Amplifies the magic significantly." Already in the fortnight since their marriage, regular, joyful lovemaking had revealed that the magic responded significantly to their bond. The hope was that the amplified magic, here at the nexus itself, would be enough to break the curse's hold.

Slowly, almost in a trance, Jacqueline and Eduard walked toward the dark, pulsing energy at the centre of the little sun-blasted vale. Once verdant, the area had been rendered not into the

118

kind of living desert that existed in the fabled east, but a dead place lifeless so long that it was hard to imagine anything ever flourishing there. Unwilling to allow his wife and queen to lie directly on the cursed land, Eduard lowered himself, stretched out on his back, and reached for her.

Chapter 13

Reality came back to me gradually, the sights and sounds of Vinzenza fading, being replaced by a wordless trance track and the familiar view from my desk of our backyard. Time for a break. Past time. I grabbed a grapefruit water on my way to Gabe's room, where I often took my breaks, feeling excitement flutter in my belly just knowing I'd be surrounded by his scent and his essence in a minute. I let myself in and curled up on his bed, cuddling his pillow to my face. Little contented sounds like purrs came from my throat. I had it bad.

As usual, it was not long before my hand drifted down my body, sneaking into my panties. After a long stint at my desk, I decided to start slow, explore every sensation, take my time. I ran a single fingertip whisper-light along the edge of my labia, up one side, down the other. Already, the flesh was enflamed and sensitive, damp with anticipation. I indulged in a long, cooing moan.

Just after deciding to repeat the process, but with two fingertips, my phone began to chirp. My breath caught, both from the surprise and from the hope that it would be Gabe. I opened the FaceTime call from him eagerly, a goofy smile on my face. "Heeey, handsome," I purred playfully when his face appeared on the screen. I was rewarded with that beautiful, cocky grin.

"Hey gorgeous," he responded with a chuckle. "How has the writing gone today? You must be almost there, right?" I could see that he was in his room, sitting up in bed. His hair looked freshly showered, and he was dressed in sweatpants and a t-shirt. The hand between my legs twitched, a mixture of wanting his hand there and wanting my hand to be on him. I gave a languorous smile.

"Almost there. Another day or two. I'll make the deadline, for sure. Might get it turned in and then just sleep for two days," I reported. "Mostly I just have their Happily Ever After to resolve and write. And how has your day been, kiddo?" We talked easily about his news and the final stages of my project, all while one hand quietly stroked and played between my legs.

"You going to tell me why you were in my room when I called, or am I going to drag it out of you," he asked finally, in a teasing tone. "You just couldn't get enough of me, is that it?" I dropped my eyes so he wouldn't see how directly he'd hit the bull's eye, too late. His tone softened. "Mir? Is that it? Is it that you can't get enough of my magic dick?" He burst into chortling laughter.

"BRAT!" I shrieked through my laughter. "I don't know why I even put up with you!" I giggled.

"Um, we just covered that, Miriam," he answered smugly. "Magic dick, remember? Speaking of which," he moved his phone, so the camera fell on his cock, hard, in one hand. My eyes went wide.

"Have you-have you been doing that this whole time?" I managed to ask. He grinned.

"The whole time," he confirmed. "And if I know my naughty lady, I'll bet you have too." My expression told him he was right. "Show me," he ordered. I moved my phone to show where my hand disappeared into my clothes. He tsked in disapproval. "No, Miriam. Show me. Please?" Adrenaline coursing through me, I figured out how to set the phone so he could see and pushed down my leggings and panties. His sharp intake of breath was deeply satisfying to me. I braced myself on my elbows and parted my legs enough to give him a show when my hand went back to work. For his benefit, I started back at the beginning, running a fingertip up and down, before dipping fingers in to pinch and pull at my clit. Knowing he was watching, and getting off on it, fuelled me, making everything I did feel more intense. Within a couple of minutes, I was panting. I allowed myself a long moan, which earned me the pleasure of a similar moan ripped from his own throat. I could see that his movements had gotten feverish, almost desperate. He must be getting close.

"You don't have a toy in there?" he asked raggedly. Actually, I did, not from today, but one I'd brought with me the other day and left here. Did I dare admit that to him, though? My hesitation sharpened his attention. "You do, don't you?" he asked excitedly. Smiling shyly, I pulled the vibrator out from under the pillow. "We're gonna talk later about how hot it is that you have that under my pillow, just in case," he gasped. "But right now, I need you to turn that on and fuck yourself with it." I did as I was bid, leaving it on the lowest setting, because I knew even with that, I would last less than a minute.

I ran the head of the vibrator along my slit to lubricate it before plunging it in my pussy with a little cry. "Fuck, Miriam, that's so hot," he moaned. I moved it faster, fucking myself with it fast and hard, my climax already starting, causing me to cry out. "Don't stop, please," he begged. I didn't. I couldn't. I was riding a crest of orgasm that I was unequal to interrupting. I cried out several more times, but didn't slow until his own cry, much quieter since he didn't have the luxury of a house to himself, told me he had climaxed. I dropped the vibrator to the bed and let my legs fold to the side, still breathing in staccato gasps. Through the phone, I could hear Gabe's breath also slowly returning to normal. I stretched like a satisfied cat, not bothering to cover myself, and smiled.

"That was a great idea, kiddo. I've always said you were an ideas man," I joked sleepily.

"Too right," he laughed. "I grew up around famous authors, you know. Raised me to be just like them." I chuckled along with him. "Hey, I gotta jet, though, Miriam. There's a study session for the Stats final I want to go to, just in case."

"Okay, Gabe. I'll let you go do that, and I'll go get cleaned up," I grinned. "Bye, kiddo."

Ten minutes after I hung up, I was still lying there on my back on Gabe's bed, grinning like a fool. Probably time to get cleaned up and get back to work after treating myself to such a nice break. I had a book to finish writing.

I forced myself to focus on Jacqueline and Eduard, and two or three hours passed before I was pulled from my intense writing by the doorbell. I almost decided to ignore it, but just in case it was a neighbour in trouble or something, I sighed and made my way to the door. Through the panel next to the door, I could see a huge floral bouquet in the hands of a delivery person. I opened the door in surprise. "Miriam?" the delivery guy asked, after consulting the clipboard.

"That's me," I said with surprise. I signed the proffered delivery confirmation and thanked the man before carrying the bouquet into the house. The bouquet was huge, a riot of roses, ranunculi, and unusual greens I didn't even know the names of. A quick hunt revealed a little card nestled among the blooms. I opened it and pulled the card out.

A wise woman once wrote that most universal rules aren't quite as universal as people think. Who needs normal? We have magic. -G

I dropped heavily into the nearest chair, my breath suddenly short. Nothing could have surprised me more than the combination of flowers and card. Well. The fact that the bouquet was unerringly chosen to suit my most precise favourites was not surprising. Gabe was one to notice such things and remember them. It was the first time he had sent me flowers, but he had been paying attention. I read and reread the card at least a hundred times, scarcely believing it was real, nor that he truly meant it. My mind struggled to process the enormity of what I held in my hands. "Who needs normal? We have magic." How on earth--? I had just written that scene the day before. There was no way Gabe could have read it. How did he know the exact words? The notes! The notes I had made that morning in his room. I'd been wondering what I did with them. Had had to reconstruct the speech from memory. He must have found them and read them.

All our confusion, all our worry about the rules, it all boiled down to this. Jacqueline and Eduard had solved the problem in my mind, and apparently, in Gabe's too. He read my thoughts on the subject, and his response was to send flowers and quote my indirect declaration back to me. I carried the flowers into my office and put them on my desk, making sure I had the best possible view of them. Hands trembling, I struggled to formulate a text to acknowledge the flowers and everything they represented. It was so big, and I was feeling so many things at once, it took far longer than its few words might have indicated. *Wow. My heart is so full. Thank you, kiddo. Call me tonight? -M*

That evening, as much to keep myself from pacing restlessly until he called as anything else, I pushed through later than usual, working hard to finish the project this week, to have it delivered before the weekend. I was bent over my keyboard, typing, deleting, thinking, fully immersed in Vinzenza and the imminent closing of the story. A throat being cleared behind me nearly made me leap out of my skin. I looked up to see Gabe reflected in the window, leaning against the doorjamb, arms crossed. "Gabe!" I cried with joy, turning to look at him.

"I see you got the flowers," he chuckled. And then, composure falling away, he closed the distance between us and pulled me out of my chair, crushing his mouth to mine. Automatically, my arms rose to wrap around him and pull him closer. For several minutes, we engaged in a hungry exchange of kisses and gasps before finally breaking apart, both of us gasping. Gabe rested his forehead against mine.

"Surprise," he murmured. "I got in the car right after my final. I should have told you, but I didn't know I was coming until I was in the car, getting on the freeway. I had to see you." His last words sent fire through my veins even more than the subsequent nip of my ear. "Is that okay?" he asked, suddenly uncertain. "I know you're almost done-" I cut him off with a long kiss.

"Don't say it," I chided. "I'm so glad you're here!" I took his hand and led him toward the kitchen, where I planned to open a bottle of wine and see what there was that we could eat. Gabe had other ideas. He took over the leading and led me down the hallway toward his room. Once inside, he started tugging at the bottom of my shirt immediately, pulling it up and over my head before tossing it aside. Groaning, he buried his face in my neck and hair. Leaving a trail of kisses along my jaw and down my neck, he reached behind me to unhook my bra, sliding the straps down my arms and tossing it in the same general direction as my shirt. He bent his head to take one nipple in his mouth, leaving the other to the attentions of one hand. I plucked impatiently at his long-sleeved t-shirt until he lifted his head from my breasts just long enough to yank the shirt over his head with a growl and toss it aside.

His hands roamed over my bare back and down to my ass. At first, he caressed me outside my leggings, cupping me and lifting until I was on my tiptoes. He kissed up to my neck and said – pleaded, really – into my ear, "Miriam, I want you. I want us to. . .Do you want that, too? Is it just me here?" He nuzzled my ear and neck, inhaling my scent, but otherwise, held himself still, waiting. Both of us breathed shallowly, leaning against each other, drawing strength from each other, knowing this was a point of no return. If we did this, did what he was suggesting, "just fooling around" was out the window, no matter what else happened, or didn't happen, in the future.

Remembering the card, "Who needs normal? We have magic," I reached for him. Resting my forehead against his chest, hands shaking, I slowly worked the end of his belt out of the loop, pulling on it to allow enough give for me to release the buckle. I fed the end out and free of the buckle. I popped the button on his jeans and drew the zipper slowly, steadily down. I cupped his hips at the sides and pushed his jeans and boxer briefs down. I bent my knees to follow them down. He lifted one foot, and then the other, to let me pull them free. I tugged his socks off at the same time, leaving him completely naked. I straightened gradually, lightly running my lips over his skin as I did. Finally, standing straight, I looked up into Gabe's face. Already, as soon as he could reach, he had hooked his thumbs in the waistband of my leggings. With excruciating slowness, he peeled them down my legs, until he pulled them off, one leg at a time. He was crouched there, his face level with the little slip of material that was the only scrap of clothing left between us. Gently, he took hold of the panties and eased them off my hips and down, down my legs until I was able to step out of them. He nuzzled my belly button and stood. There we stood, completely naked, in his room, right next to his bed. We stared into each other's eyes.

Hesitantly, reverently, Gabe brought his mouth to mine. I felt that we had already crossed the point of no return and there was nothing left to hold us back. When his lips met mine, every kiss we'd shared, every touch we'd exchanged, every gasp we'd drawn from each other reverberated through me all at once, firing my blood, giving me both the courage and the bone-shaking *need* to do what came next. "Gabe," I whispered into his mouth. I reached for him, needing him closer. He crushed me to him, his cock between us, hot and hard against my stomach. I could feel the first drops of his moisture on my skin, presaging a release coming for both of us unlike any we had had before.

We had taken the last few steps to the bed. I felt it hit the backs of my legs. I let my legs fold, sat, scooted back onto the bed to make room for Gabe. He followed readily, crawling onto the bed, crawling over me, holding himself above me. I reached up to gather him to me. My legs fell open to make room for him between them. He stroked my flank, kissing now my face, now my breasts. "Miriam," he moaned. "Mir. Fuck. Yes, oh, God." He lay on top of me, the head of his cock resting at my entrance, my legs cradling his hips.

128

"Now, Gabe. I'm ready," I urged. He looked into my eyes, hesitated only briefly, and pushed into me in one, slow, smooth thrust. He filled me, stretched me, felt absolutely perfect inside me. We stared into each other's eyes while he stroked into me again and again, electrifying the air around us. I was suffused with a sense that I was home in a way I never had been before. It was so simple and perfect for Gabe to be inside me. I brought my legs up around his waist, opening me and pulling him in further.

"Miriam," he panted. "I have to stop, or, well, I have to stop this for a minute. And I need to taste you." I whimpered regretfully when he eased out of me, but his hand promptly moved in to lessen the sting of need. My facial expression must have reflected the disappointment and subsequent relief. He grinned smugly. "Don't worry, gorgeous," he teased. "I'll make you feel good."

He kissed me sweetly, and then began to kiss a path down my body, while his hand continued to play between my legs as if I were an instrument, and he was determined to coax the most beautiful music from me. I buried my fingers in his hair and sighed contentedly. He nuzzled and kissed my breasts, lightly biting and licking first one nipple, then the other. He had my clit between two fingers, running them along it, pinching just enough to heighten the sensation, making it swell with blood. I writhed in sweet torment under his ministrations. I might have groaned when he left my nipples to move further down, were it not for the delicious anticipation of what was yet to come. Gabe peppered playful kisses here and there on my stomach as he backed further down the bed, eliciting from me delighted giggles. My giggles were rewarded when Gabe plunged two fingers into me, their thrusts punctuating my gasps.

His mouth reached my mound, and a low moan escaped me. Gabe settled himself on his knees between my legs, leaving both hands free now to play. He used his fingers to spread me open and lowered his head to thrust his tongue into my slit right at my entrance, before running his tongue upward along the length of my slit until he got to my sensitive clit. Tenderly, he took the swollen bud into his mouth, holding it gently in place between his teeth while his tongue swirled around it over and over. My hips came up off the mattress. I cried out, grinding my pussy against Gabe's face as hard as I could. As the orgasm broke over me, I instinctively tried to escape the surfeit of intense sensation, but Gabe pursued me as I backed up the bed. His mouth and hands followed me, relentless, though he gentled his treatment of my enflamed clit.

I opened my eyes to look at Gabe in wonder. "Kiddo," I gasped. "That. . ." my breath was still coming in staccato gasps. My orgasm-addled attempt to describe it was interrupted by Gabe sinking back into me. He let more of his weight rest against me, pushing hard into me. A long, low moan rumbled out of my beautiful, sexy Gabe. He braced himself on his elbows and thrust deep into me, harder than before, and faster.

I gripped Gabe by the shoulders to still him. I didn't bring my legs back up around him. "Gabe," I said, urgently, to get his attention. "I need you under me. Roll over," I ordered. His eyes widened. He grinned and complied, treating me to a sexy chuckle while he watched me climb on top of him. I straddled him, reached between us to put him in position, and slowly impaled myself on him. In this position, it felt like taking all of him might split me in half, and I loved it.

Bracing myself on Gabe's chest, I started to ride him, slowly at first. He gripped my hips and met me thrust for thrust, his face a study in concentration. Another orgasm gathered itself in my body, waiting, but not for long, to unleash itself in me. My breathing told Gabe it was building. His fingers tightened on my hips. "Yes, Miriam, again, come with me," he urged. His thrusts got harder. He used his hands to pull me onto him harder with every thrust. He whimpered quietly, overwhelmed by the sensations building inside him. "Fuck, Miriam. Yes, yessss." With a final thrust up into me, he held me in place on him, come pumping out of him into me, which pushed me over the edge. I squeezed him hard from inside and cried out from the intensity of our shared orgasm. My whole body was rigid with it. I collapsed on his chest.

Gabe rolled us onto our sides, facing each other. He kissed both of my cheeks, my forehead, my nose, and then, with aching sweetness, my lips. "Miriam," he murmured. "My gorgeous-" *Kiss.* "Sweet-" *Kiss.* "Talented-" *Kiss.* "Miriam." He chuckled. "Mine," he concluded, gathering me into his arms.

"Mmmhmm," I agreed sleepily. "My magic boy." And I slept, a contented smile on my face.

I awoke to Gabe calling to me. "Miriam," he said with a grin when he saw my eyes open. "Your stomach is growling," he laughed. "We better get something to eat." With any other lover, this would have been cause for embarrassment, but with Gabe, I was able to giggle, not at all self-conscious.

"Yeah, now you mention it," I confirmed, "I'm starving." I tossed him a lascivious grin and swung my legs over him to crawl backward off the bed. He stood and pulled me to him before I could pull on the shirt I had retrieved from the floor. He bent to kiss me. I happily returned the kiss, dropping the shirt to wrap my arms around him.

"Oh no, you don't," he laughed, gently pushing me from him. "Food first. I can't have you collapsing from exhaustion because you're too absorbed with fucking me to eat." He chuckled, sweet and cocky and perfect.

"Brat!" I shrieked, snatching up the pillow from the bed and raising it to wallop him. Gabe pinned my arms to my sides with a bear hug and kissed my nose.

"Tsk tsk, roomie," he chided playfully. "No violence before dinner. House rule." I struggled in his embrace, laughing.

"Fine, fine, okay, brat," I conceded. "Let's get some dinner, so I can fuck you again." His arms loosened, letting me bend the gather my shirt back up. I slid it on and stepped into my panties. I left my bra and leggings where they were and headed for the kitchen. Gabe walked in behind me in boxer briefs, still pulling his shirt on. He went straight to the fridge and started pulling out eggs, milk, butter, and cheese.

"Omelette?" he asked. I nodded and got out herbs and a pepper to add to it. For several minutes, we worked in comfortable quiet, both of us knowing the motions of a last-minute omelette dinner by heart through our two years' of habit. Gabe slid the omelette halves onto plates while I poured two glasses of white wine to go with the meal. I settled there at the counter and waited for Gabe to sit before starting to eat.

"Mmm, nice job, kiddo, this might be the best one you've ever made," I congratulated him. He flashed me his wolfish grin.

"Yeah, well, I've never made an omelette after making love to a gorgeous woman before. I guess it gives me superpowers." He leaned over to kiss the tip of my nose. "So, the book, is it finished?"

"Almost," I replied, relieved that it was true. "I just have a couple of chapters left."

"We can go in there after we eat and I can keep you company while you write," he offered.

"I couldn't ask you to do that, Gabe. I can finish tomorrow." He put his glass down and pulled me to him, bending to kiss my nose.

"But think about this. I'm done with finals and I have three days before I fly out for Christmas. So, if you finish that tonight, we can spend all day tomorrow in bed. Together." A light kiss turned searing and greedy. We were both breathing heavily when we broke apart.

"You make a compelling argument, kiddo," I grinned.

"I know," he responded, taking my plate and carrying it to the sink. "Come on, let's go get this finished."

We headed to the office hand in hand. The idea of writing the final scenes of Jacqueline and Eduard's story, which had been so important in opening me to the amazing thing I was building with Gabe, with him in the room, was appealing and exciting.

It was a struggle, forcing myself into the lives of Jacqueline and Eduard, writing their struggle, their happy ending, when Gabe was close enough that my arm could feel the heat radiating from his body. Gradually, through force of will, I immersed myself into the story, embodying my characters and shaping their fates as a benevolent goddess. I was aware of Gabe glancing over. I was always aware of him, but now. . .

I was deep in Jacqueline's and Eduard's breaking of the curse when I felt Gabe at my shoulder. I glanced at him, my eyebrow raised. The fire in his eyes told me he had been reading the scene and was not unaffected by Eduard's attention to Jacqueline's comfort as he settled himself on the cursed ground and reached for her. "Shh," he offered, chuckling, "Don't mind me. Just reading over your shoulder. Is that okay?" My eyes, of their own accord, dropped to his lips. His beautiful lips. Warm and inviting. . . "Mir, focus." He chuckled, lowering his head to nuzzle my neck. "I'm just reading over your shoulder. No need to look at me like I'm a buffet." Belying his words, his arm snaked around my abdomen to pull us closer. He started trailing kisses along my shoulder. "Tell me what they're up to now, Mir, give me the context for this part," he urged, even as he made it nigh impossible for my heated mind to process English intelligently.

"Really?" I asked uncertainly. He allowed himself a leisurely suckle at my right ear lobe before answering.

"Yeah, really. Tell me what they're up to. Last I knew, the queen and a young nobleman had to get married and," here he paused to roll his chair around the back of mine to give him access to the other side of my neck. "And have sex to lift the curse, right?" His words came to me through a descending fog of desire. It took some time to process the words.

"Um. . . yeah, so they, oh God, Gabe, . . .they got married. Then they had to figure out how to break. . .Oooh, kiddo..." I moaned.

"Don't stop, Miriam. Keep telling me," he urged, before burying his face in my hair and cradling my head against his lips. One hand snaked up under my t-shirt to trace figures idly on my abdomen. I let my head rest against his hand and felt my eyes roll into the back of my head. Another moan escaped me.

"After they married at Eduard's birthday feast celebrating his coming into his majority, they consummated the marriage in front of some Order members, because they were pushed to. It went better than expected." I went on, "They gathered their allies close and conceived of a plan to break the curse without the help of the Order, to circumvent their power. Oh, Gabe, please don't stop," I begged, gripping the arms of my chair. His hand had moved up further to cup one breast and was idly playing with the tightening bud of my nipple. It was all I could do not to launch myself at him.

Gabe studiously pulled my shirt to the side with his other hand, to expose my shoulder. "Keep talking," he murmured against my bare shoulder. "How do they break the curse?" His fingers played along my arm while he traced my shoulder with tiny, sweet kisses. I drew in my breath sharply.

"Gabe," I whispered. My body shifted toward him, eager for him. He abruptly stopped and raised his eyes to mine. He grinned mischievously, seeing the hunger in my own eyes, and withdrew his hands from me, my only consolation that he very obviously hated the sanction as much as I.

"Naughty Miriam," he said with playful severity. "I specifically told you to keep telling the story." He walked his fingers back down my arm while he spoke, leaning closer. "You don't want me to stop touching you, do you?"

"No, please, no," I confirmed. He nuzzled my ear and chuckled in response.

"Good," he agreed, "Because I'm not going anywhere."

"Gabe, I want..." his lips on my throat cut off whatever I had been about to say.

"Mmmm? Yes? You want what, Miriam?" he murmured.

"Maybe, I could take a break to, um...gather inspiration," I gasped, biting my lip when he pinched my nipple mischievously.

"I have a better idea," he said, grinning. "You. . . gather inspiration and tell me the story while you do. I'll take dictation." Challenge and glee glinted in his eye.

"What, you mean-" I blushed, which was admittedly a bit rich from the woman who was fucking a kid half her age. "You mean, in here? Just. . .?"

He turned the full force of his gaze on me. "Yes, Miriam. I want you to sit next to me, right here, and touch yourself while you dictate this scene to me. Will you do that?" My mouth dry, eyes locked on his, I pulled him to me for a long, slow kiss. I let my hand trail from where it cupped his neck down his arm to where his hand rested on my hip. Biting my lip, I let my hand slide from where it covered his to move between my thighs. His eyes dropped to watch it hungrily.

"Okay, kiddo," I said shakily. "You ready?" He hesitated. I could tell he was questioning the wisdom of his plan and thinking about abandoning the idea. "Gabe? You ready?" He tore his eyes from where I was slowly stroking myself.

"I...yes." He cleared his throat. He turned to the keyboard reluctantly, stealing glances over at me. Gathering my thoughts, I considered where I had left Eduard and Jacqueline. Not wanting her to lie on the cursed ground if she didn't have to, he had lain down and held up his arms to her. Sitting next to Gabe, my arm touching his arm, my hand exploring the damp folds between my legs, I closed my eyes and brought forth the image. The burned earth. The searing wind. Eduard reaching up for Jacqueline with both arms, trusting, open. Jacqueline looking down at him with such love, feeling so amazed at how things had taken shape since the wedding.

Chapter 14

Overwhelmed by love and hope, Jacqueline loosened the belt that held her gown closed and let the gown fall open. Eyes locked with Eduard's, she lowered herself to cover him. He received her tenderly, kissing her deeply as he folded her into his arms. The scant magic they had spooled flared between them and grew, pulsing into a life of its own. Eduard, looking up, saw the changing magic and gaped. "It's never done this before," he murmured against Jacqueline's hair. "Do you think it's a good sign?" The consensus among the sovereigns' allies was that any amplification of their magic for the ritual was to be desired. The queen fervently hoped they were right. If the curse wasn't broken on the first attempt, the Order's influence would be strengthened in its cold war against the thrones. More worrying was the possibility that this close to the nexus of the curse, the magic might somehow be perverted to harm or twist its wielders. There were no records of any precedent, since there had never before been two simultaneous magic-wielding sovereigns. No amount of research would inform that aspect of the attempt. They must try, they must support each other, and they must be watchful for any aberrance in the magic.

The pulsing growth of the magic seemed aberrance enough, but not malevolent. "It still feels right, to me," the queen commented. "Only...bigger, more alive." Eduard took a moment to experience the magic and examine its changed qualities.

"I think it still feels right," he agreed. "Perhaps it's already responding to our coupling, even though we've only just started?" He punctuated his conjecture by gripping Jacqueline's hip with one hand and reaching between their bodies to pull at the ties at his waist. "Do you think we should-" In answer, his wife reached in to free him from his clothing and gave him a firm stroke to gauge his readiness before guiding him to her opening.

"Yes," she urged. "Now. The time for leisurely lovemaking will be in our chambers later, in celebration of the breaking of the curse." She kissed him, pouring all the hope and desire for relief from the curse into the kiss as they pressed their bodies together so that he entered her. "Eduard," she gasped, amazed anew at the rightness of having him fill her. The magic pulsed again, and again, taking on the rhythm and cadence of a heartbeat. Was it a heartbeat? The heartbeat of the land, coming back to life? The queen rode her young husband's body, watching and listening to the magic growing, overtaking the power of the curse, gathering to restore life to the land.

Lost in each other and the magic, they moved ever faster, came together ever more forcefully, enjoying the coupling but keenly aware of the vital importance of its success. The magic surrounded them with tangible density now, its beating causing the earth to tremble. "My love," warned Eduard, "Do you think-? Should I-"

Jacqueline's gaze was suffused with her love and passion for her husband and for their land. "Together, love," she moaned. "We will do cross over together. Oh, Eduard, the magic, it's working, yes, it's time, love. It's time." She cried out with her climax just as he did with his own, a burst of blindingly bright magic blasting out from their joined bodies to bathe the land in light and warmth. Gasping in each other's arms, tears streaming down their faces, they watched in awe as the land under and around them started to come to life before their eyes.

"It worked," Eduard whispered, reverent. "It worked. We did it. We broke the curse." His voice grew in confidence as the reality settled upon him. The curse that had plagued the kingdom since long before either of them was born was gone, broken by their union, his unexpectedly joyful union with his queen, his wife. Grinning, he hooked a foot behind Jacqueline's knee and rolled them, putting her underneath him. She laughed while he showered her face with kisses. "We broke the curse," he repeated again and again. "We broke the curse." He pushed into her again, taking time for a more leisurely, celebratory lovemaking than he'd believed he'd be indulging in so soon. The queen received him enthusiastically, pulling him into her and planting kisses everywhere she could reach. They made love there for hours before, exhausted, they rose and covered themselves enough to make the journey home for the announcement, which would be unnecessary, since the curse's demise would be apparent everywhere already.

Chapter 15

Gabe looked up from the breast he had been kissing. "Is that where that part ends, and the epilogue you wrote starts? Should I stop the recording?" Somehow as I'd narrated the conclusion, Gabe had convinced me to let him record the narration, promising to transcribe it for me later, so that we could move into the bedroom to be more comfortable, as he put it. I had to admit, narrating a sex scene while having my body touched and kissed had been a beautiful experience, and one I hoped we would reprise.

"That's the end of that chapter," I confirmed. "From there, it goes to the epilogue."

"Why did you write the epilogue before the rest was finished? You don't always do that, do you?" He'd been watching writers for years. I was proud that he understood that this was a deviation from my usual writing practice.

"Well, in this case, I knew where I wanted them to be, and I wanted to establish that horizon in my mind," I responded after a moment's consideration. "I knew I wanted them to have broken the curse, without anything bad happening to either of them. More importantly, in terms of writing the epilogue early, I didn't know yet what kinds of challenges their relationship was going to face over the course of the story, but I knew I wanted them to end up happy, together, and without shame." Gabe looked at me intently.

"Happy, together, and without shame," he repeated thoughtfully. "Did you write the epilogue before we started..." He spent his hand through the air parallel to our bodies. "Before this?" he finished.

I thought a moment. "I wrote the epilogue the day I came home from seeing you at Family Weekend. We had gone pretty far, and I had sort of masqueraded as your girlfriend, and... my mind was full of us. I didn't know what was going to happen, but I knew it would be founded in our affection for each other and I knew I wanted it to be free from shame. That's important to me, whatever happens."

He moved up to lie next to me, rolling me so we were face to face. "I've thought about it so much," he began, his words deliberate. "I-I agree, we can't live with shame. There will be people who judge sometimes. You're utterly gorgeous but we don't look the same age. They'll try to shame us, but your words, about universal rules not being universal, really unlocked it for me." He started to trace my facial features with a finger. "I don't pretend to understand why, or how, but you're it for me, Miriam. I don't want anyone else." Both of us had tears streaming down our faces. He kissed me sweetly, fingers tangling in my hair. I deepened the kiss, hungry for him, deliriously happy at the implications of what he had just said. So hungry and so happy, it took me a moment to realize when he gently gripped my shoulder and pushed us apart. I scowled in confusion. "I, um, I need to know if we're, you know, in agreement there," he said. There was terrible uncertainty in his expression.

143

"Gabe, I don't know why this happened with us." I tangled our legs together and scooted closer. "But I'm glad it did. Yes, I'm yours, completely. I want us to be together. Free from shame. Now kiss me again, brat. You made me keep working, and I appreciate it, but now I need you in me." He chuckled and rolled on top of me.

"As my queen commands," he grinned, and lowered his lips to mine.

THE END

www.ingramcontent.com/pod-product-compliance
Lightning Source LLC
Chambersburg PA
CBHW011513170626
46810CB00009B/3349